The Melody of Death

The Melody of Death

Edgar Wallace

MINT EDITIONS

The Melody of Death was first published in 1915.

This edition published by Mint Editions 2021.

ISBN 9781513280820 | E-ISBN 9781513285849

Published by Mint Editions®

 MINT
EDITIONS

minteditionbooks.com

Publishing Director: Jennifer Newens
Design & Production: Rachel Lopez Metzger
Project Manager: Micaela Clark
Typesetting: Westchester Publishing Services

Table of Contents

I

The Amateur Safe Smasher

On the night of May 27, 1911, the office of Gilderheim, Pascoe and Company, diamond merchants, of Little Hatton Garden, presented no unusual appearance to the patrolling constable who examined the lock and tried the door in the ordinary course of his duty. Until nine o'clock in the evening the office had been occupied by Mr. Gilderheim and his head clerk, and a plain-clothes officer, whose duty was to inquire into unusual happenings, had deemed that the light in the window on the first floor fell within his scope, and had gone up to discover the reason for its appearance. The 27th was a Saturday, and it is usual for the offices in Hatton Garden to be clear of clerks and their principals by three at the latest.

Mr. Gilderheim, a pleasant gentleman, had been relieved to discover that the knock which brought him to the door, gripping a revolver in his pocket in case of accidents, produced no more startling adventure than a chat with a police officer who was known to him. He explained that he had to-day received a parcel of diamonds from an Amsterdam house, and was classifying the stones before leaving for the night, and with a few jocular remarks on the temptation which sixty thousand pounds' worth of diamonds offered to the unscrupulous "night of darkness," the officer left.

At nine-forty Mr. Gilderheim locked up the jewels in his big safe, before which an electric light burnt day and night, and accompanied by his clerk, left No. 93 Little Hatton Garden and walked in the direction of Holborn.

The constable on point duty bade them good-night, and the plain-clothes officer who was then at the Holborn end of the thoroughfare, exchanged a word or two.

"You will be on duty all night?" asked Mr. Gilderheim as his clerk hailed a cab.

"Yes, sir," said the officer.

"Good!" said the merchant. "I'd like you to keep a special eye upon my place. I am rather nervous about leaving so large a sum in the safe."

The officer smiled.

"I don't think you need worry, sir," he said; and, after the cab containing Mr. Gilderheim had driven off he walked back to No. 93.

But in that brief space of time between the diamond merchant leaving and the return of the detective many things had happened. Scarcely had Gilderheim reached the detective than two men walked briskly along the thoroughfare from the other end. Without hesitation the first turned into No. 93, opened the door with a key, and passed in. The second man followed. There was no hesitation, nothing furtive in their movements. They might have been lifelong tenants of the house, so confident were they in every action.

Not half a minute after the second man had entered a third came from the same direction, turned into the building, unlocked the door with that calm confidence which had distinguished the action of the first comer, and went in.

Three minutes later two of the three were upstairs. With extraordinary expedition one had produced two small iron bottles from his pockets and had deftly fixed the rubber tubes and adjusted the little blow-pipe of his lamp, and the second had spread out on the floor a small kit of tools of delicate temper and beautiful finish.

Neither man spoke. They lay flat on the ground, making no attempt to extinguish the light which shone before the safe. They worked in silence for some little while, then the stouter of the two remarked, looking up at the reflector fixed at an angle to the ceiling and affording a view of the upper part of the safe to the passer-by in the street below:

"Even the mirrors do not give us away, I suppose?"

The second burglar was a slight, young-looking man with a shock of hair that suggested the musician. He shook his head.

"Unless all the rules of optics have been specially reversed for the occasion," he said with just a trace of a foreign accent, "we cannot possibly be seen."

"I am relieved," said the first.

He half whistled, half hummed a little tune to himself as he plied the hissing flame to the steel door.

He was carefully burning out the lock, and had no doubt in his mind that he would succeed, for the safe was an old-fashioned one. No further word was exchanged for half an hour. The man with the blow-pipe continued in his work, the other watching with silent interest, ready to play his part when the operation was sufficiently advanced.

At the end of half an hour the elder of the two wiped his streaming forehead with the back of his hand, for the heat which the flame gave back from the steel door was fairly trying.

"Why did you make such a row closing the door?" he asked. "You are not usually so careless, Calli."

The other looked down at him in mild astonishment.

"I made no noise whatever, my dear George," he said. "If you had been standing in the passage you could not have heard it; in fact, I closed the door as noiselessly as I opened it."

The perspiring man on the ground smiled.

"That would be fairly noiseless," he said.

"Why?" asked the other.

"Because I did not close it. You walked in after me."

Something in the silence which greeted his words made him look up. There was a puzzled look upon his companion's face.

"I opened the door with my own key," said the younger man slowly.

"You opened—" The man called George frowned. "I do not understand you, Callidino. I left the door open, and you walked in after me; I went straight up the stairs, and you followed."

Callidino looked at the other and shook his head.

"I opened the door myself with the key," he said quietly. "If anybody came in after you—why, it is up to us, George, to see who it is."

"You mean—?"

"I mean," said the little Italian, "that it would be extremely awkward if there is a third gentleman present on this inconvenient occasion."

"It would, indeed," said the other.

"Why?"

Both men turned with a start, for the voice that asked the question without any trace of emotion was the voice of a third man, and he stood in the doorway screened from all possibility of observation from the window by the angle of the room.

He was dressed in an evening suit, and he carried a light overcoat across his arm.

What manner of man he was, and how he looked, they had no means of judging, for from his chin to his forehead his face was covered by a black mask.

"Please do not move," he said, "and do not regard the revolver I am holding in the light of a menace. I merely carry it for self-defence, and you will admit that under the circumstances and knowing the extreme delicacy of my position, I am fairly well justified in taking this precaution."

George Wallis laughed a little under his breath.

"Sir," he said, without shifting his position "you may be a man after my own heart, but I shall know better when you have told me exactly what you want."

"I want to learn," said the stranger. He stood there regarding the pair with obvious interest. The eyes which shone through the holes of the mask were alive and keen. "Go on with your work, please," he said. "I should hate to interrupt you."

George Wallis picked up the blow-pipe and addressed himself again to the safe door. He was a most adaptable man, and the situation in which he found himself nonplussed had yet to occur.

"Since," he said, "it makes absolutely no difference as to whether I leave off or whether I go on, if you are a representative of law and order, I may as well go on, because if you are not a representative of those two admirable, excellent and necessary qualities I might at least save half the swag with you."

"You may save the lot," said the man sharply. "I do not wish to share the proceeds of your robbery, but I want to know how you do it—that is all."

"You shall learn," said George Wallis, that most notorious of burglars, "and at the hands of an expert, I beg you to believe."

"That I know," said the other calmly.

Wallis went on with his task apparently undisturbed by this extraordinary interruption. The little Italian's hands had twitched nervously, and here might have been trouble, but the strength of the other man, who was evidently the leader of the two, and his self-possession had heartened his companion to accept whatever consequences the presence of this man might threaten. It was the masked stranger who broke the silence.

"Isn't it an extraordinary thing," he said, "that whilst technical schools exist for teaching every kind of trade, art and craft, there is none which engage in teaching the art of destruction. Believe me, I am very grateful that I have had this opportunity of sitting at the feet of a master."

His voice was not unpleasant, but there was a certain hardness which was not in harmony with the flippant tone he adopted.

The man on the floor went on with his work for a little while, then he said without turning his head:

"I am anxious to know exactly how you got in."

"I followed close behind you," said the masked man. "I knew there would be a reasonable interval between the two of you. You see," he went on, "you have been watching this office for the greater part of a week; one of you has been on duty practically every night. You rented a small office higher up this street which offered a view of these premises. I gathered that you had chosen to-night because you brought your gas with you this morning. You were waiting in the dark hallway of the building in which your office is situated, one of you watching for the light to go out and Mr. Gilderheim depart. When he had gone, you, sir"—he addressed the man on the floor—"came out immediately, your companion did not follow so soon. Moreover, he stopped to pick up a small bundle of letters which had apparently been dropped by some careless person, and since these letters included two sealed packets such as the merchants of Hatton Garden send to their clients, I was able to escape the observation of the second man and keep reasonably close to you."

Callidino laughed softly.

"That is true," he said, with a nod to the man on the floor. "It was very clever. I suppose you dropped the packet?"

The masked man inclined his head.

"Please go on," he said, "do not let me interrupt you."

"What is going to happen when I have finished?" asked George, still keeping his face to the safe.

"As far as I am concerned, nothing. Just as soon as you have got through your work, and have extracted whatever booty there is to be extracted, I shall retire."

"You want your share, I suppose?"

"Not at all," said the other calmly. "I do not want my share by any means. I am not entitled to it. My position in society prevents me from going farther down the slippery path than to connive at your larceny."

"Felony," corrected the man on the floor.

"Felony," agreed the other. He waited until without a sound the heavy door of the safe swung open and George had put his hand inside to extract the contents, and then, without a word, he passed through the door, closing it behind him. The two men sat up tensely, and listened. They heard nothing more until the soft thud of the outer door told them that their remarkable visitor had departed.

They exchanged glances—interest on the one face, amusement on the other.

"That is a remarkable man," said Callidino.

The other nodded.

"Most remarkable," he said, "and more remarkable will it be if we get out of Hatton Garden to-night with the loot."

It would seem that the "more than most" remarkable happening of all actually occurred, for none saw the jewel thieves go, and the smashing of Gilderheim's jewel safe provided an excellent alternative topic for conversation to the prospects of Sunstar for the Derby.

II

Sunstar's Derby

There it was again! Above the babel of sound, the low roar of voices, soft and sorrowful, now heard, now lost, a vagrant thread of gold caught in the drab woof of shoddy life gleaming and vanishing. . . Gilbert Standerton sat tensely straining to locate the sound.

It was the "Melody in F" that the unseen musician played.

"There's going to be a storm."

Gilbert did not hear the voice. He sat on the box-seat of the coach, clasping his knees, the perspiration streaming from his face.

There was something tragic, something a little terrifying in his pose. The profile turned to his exasperated friend was a perfect one—forehead high and well-shaped, the nose a little long, perhaps, the chin strong and resolute.

Leslie Frankfort, looking up at the unconscious dreamer, was reminded of the Dante of convention, though Dante never wore a top-hat or found a Derby Day crowd so entirely absorbing.

"There's going to be a storm." Leslie climbed up the short step-ladder, and swung himself into the seat by Gilbert's side.

The other awoke from his reverie with a start.

"Is there?" he asked, and wiped his forehead. Yet as he looked around it was not the murky clouds banking up over Banstead that held his eye; it was this packed mass of men and women, these gay placards extolling loudly the honesty and the establishment of "the old firm," the booths on the hill, the long succession of canvas screens which had. been erected to advertise somebody's whisky, the flimsy-looking stands on the far side of the course, the bustle, the pandemonium and the vitality of that vast, uncountable throng made such things as June thunderstorms of little importance.

"If you only knew how the low-brows are pitying you," said Leslie Frankfort, with good-natured annoyance, "you would not be posing for a picture of 'The Ruined Gambler.' My dear chap, you look for all the world, sitting up here with your long, ugly mug a-droop, like a model for the coloured plate to be issued with the Christmas number of the *Anti-Gambling Gazette*. I suppose they have a gazette."

Gilbert laughed a little.

"These people interest me," he said, rousing himself to speak. "Don't you realize what they all mean? Every one of them with a separate and distinct individuality, every one with a hope or a fear hugged tight in his bosom, every one with the capacity for love, or hate, or sorrow. Look at that man!" he said, and pointed with his long nervous finger.

The man he indicated stood in a little oasis of green. Hereabouts the people on the course had so directed their movements as to leave an open space, and in the centre stood a man of medium height, a black bowler on the back of his head, a long, thin cigar between his white even teeth. He was too far away for Leslie to distinguish these particulars, but Gilbert Standerton's imagination filled in the deficiencies of vision, for he had seen this man before.

As if conscious of the scrutiny, the man turned and came slowly towards the rails where the coach stood. He took the cigar from his mouth and smiled as he recognized the occupant of the box-seat.

"How do you do, sir?" His voice sounded shrill and faint, as if an immeasurably distance separated them, but he was evidently shouting to raise his voice above the growling voices of the crowd. Gilbert waved his hand with a smile; the man turned and raised his hat, and was swallowed up in a detachment of the crowd which came eddying about him.

"A thief," said Gilbert "on a fairly large scale—his name is Wallis; there are many Wallises here. A crowd is a terrible spectacle to the man who thinks," he said, half to himself.

The other glanced at him keenly.

"They're terrible things to get through in a thunderstorm," he said, practically. "I vote we go along and claim the car."

Gilbert nodded.

He rose stiffly, like a man with cramp, and stepped slowly down the little ladder to the ground. They passed through the barrier and crossed the course, penetrated the little unsaddling enclosure, through the long passages where pressmen, jockeys and stewards jostled one another every moment of race days, to the roadway without.

In the roped garage they found their car, and, more remarkable, their chauffeur.

The first flicker of blue lightning had stabbed twice to the Downs, and the heralding crash of thunder had reverberated through the charged air, when the car began to thread the traffic towards London.

The storm, which had been brewing all the afternoon broke with terrific fury over Epsom. The lightning was incessant, the rain streamed down in an almost solid wall of water, crash after crash of thunder deafened them.

The great throng upon the hill was dissolving as though it was something soluble; its edges frayed into long black streamers of hurrying people moving towards the three railway stations. It required more than ordinary agility to extricate the car from the chaos of charabancs and motor-cabs in which it found itself.

Standerton had taken his seat by the driver's side, though the car was a closed one. He was a man quick to observe, and on the second flash he had seen the chauffeur's face grow white and his lips twitching. A darkness almost as of night covered the heavens. The horizon about was rimmed with a dull, angry orange haze; so terrifying a storm had not been witnessed in England for many years.

The rain was coming down in sheets, but the young man by the chauffeur's side paid no heed. He was watching the nervous hands of the man twist this way and that as the car made detour after detour to avoid the congested road. Suddenly a jagged streak of light flicked before the car, and Standerton was deafened by an explosion more terrifying than any of the previous peals.

The chauffeur instinctively shrank back, his face white and drawn; his trembling hands left the wheel, and his foot released the pedal. The car would have come to a standstill, but for the fact that they were at the top of a declivity.

"My God!" he whimpered, "it's awful. I can't go on, sir." Gilbert Standerton's hand was on the wheel, his neatly-booted foot had closed on the brake pedal.

"Get out of it!" he muttered. "Get over here, quick!"

The man obeyed. He moved, shivering, to his master's place, his hands before his face, and Standerton slipped into the driver's seat and threw in the clutch. It was fortunate that he was a driver of extraordinary ability, but he needed every scrap of knowledge as he put the car to the slope which led to the lumpy Downs. As they jolted forward the downpour increased, the ground was running with water as though it had been recently flooded The wheels of the car slipped and skidded over the greasy surface, but the man at the steering-wheel kept his head, and by and by he brought the big car slithering down a little slope on to the main way again. The road was sprinkled with hurrying, tramping people. He moved forward slowly, his horn sounding all the time, and then of a sudden the car stopped with a jerk.

"What is it?"

Leslie Frankfort had opened the window which separated the driver's seat from the occupants of the car.

"There's an old chap there," said Gilbert, speaking over his shoulder, "would you mind taking him into the car? I'll tell you why after." He pointed to two woe-begone figures that stood on the side of the road. They were of an old man and a girl; Leslie could not see their faces distinctly. They stood with their backs to the storm, one thin coat spread about them both.

Gilbert shouted something, and at his voice the old man turned. He had a beautiful face, thin, refined, intellectual: it was the face of an artist. His grey hair straggled over his collar, and under the cloak he clutched something, the care of which seemed to concern him more than his protection from the merciless downpour.

The girl at his side might have been seventeen, a solemn child, with great fearless eyes that surveyed the occupants of the car gravely. The old man hesitated at Gilbert's invitation, but as he beckoned impatiently he brought the girl down to the road and Leslie opened the door.

"Jump in quickly," he said. "My word, you're wet!"

He slammed the door behind them, and they seated themselves facing him. They were in a pitiable condition; the girl's dress was soaked, her face was wet as though she had come straight from a bath.

"Take that cloak off," said Leslie brusquely. "I've a couple of dry handkerchiefs, though I'm afraid you'll want a bath towel."

She smiled. "It's very kind of you," she said. "We shall ruin your car."

"Oh, that's all right," said Leslie cheerfully. "It's not my car. Anyway," he added, "when Mr. Standerton comes in he will make it much worse." He was wondering in his mind by what freakish inclination Standerton had called these two people to the refuge of his limousine.

The old man smiled as he spoke, and his first words were an explanation.

"Mr. Standerton has always been very good to me," he said gently, almost humbly. He had a soft, well-modulated voice. Leslie Frankfort recognized that it was the voice of an educated man. He smiled. He was too used to meeting Standerton's friends to be surprised at this storm-soddened street musician, for such he judged him to be by the neck of the violin which protruded from the soaked coat.

"You know him, do you?" The old man nodded.

"I know him very well," he said.

He took from under his coat the thing he had been carrying, and Leslie Frankfort saw that it was an old violin. The old man examined it anxiously, then with a sigh of relief he laid it across his knees.

"It's not damaged, I hope?" asked Leslie.

"No, sir," said the other; "I was greatly afraid that it was going to be an unfortunate ending to what had been a prosperous day."

They had been playing on the Downs, and had reaped a profitable harvest.

"My grand-daughter also plays," said the old man. "We do not as a rule care for these great crowds, but it invariably means money"—he smiled—"and we are not in a position to reject any opportunity which offers."

They were now drawing clear of the storm. They had passed through Sutton, and had reached a place where the roads were as yet dry, when Gilbert stopped the car and handed the wheel to the shame-faced chauffeur.

"I'm very sorry, sir," the man began.

"Oh, don't bother," smiled his employer; "one is never to be blamed for funking a storm. I used to be as bad until I got over it. . . there are worse things," he added, half to himself.

The man thanked him with a muttered word, and Gilbert opened the door of the car and entered. He nodded to the old man and gave a quick smile to the girl. "

"I thought I recognized you," he said. "This is Mr. Springs," he said, turning to Leslie. "He's quite an old friend of mine. I'm sure when you have dined at St. John's Wood you must have heard Springs' violin under the dining-room window. It used to be a standing order, didn't it, Mr. Springs?" he said. "By the way," he asked suddenly, "were you playing—"

He stopped, and the old man, misunderstanding the purport of the question, nodded.

"After all," said Gilbert, with a sudden change of manner, "it wouldn't be humane to leave my private band to drown on Epsom Downs, to say nothing of the chance of his being struck by lightning."

"Was there any danger?" asked Leslie in surprise.

Gilbert nodded.

"I saw one poor chap struck as I cleared the Downs," he said; "there were a lot of people near him, so I didn't trouble to stop. It was a terrifying experience." He looked back out of the little oval window behind.

"We shall have it again in London to-night," he said, "but storms do not feel so dangerous in town as they do in the country. They're not so alarming. Housetops are very merciful to the nervous."

They took farewell of the old man and his grand-daughter at Balham, and then, as the car continued, Leslie turned with a puzzled look to his companion.

"You're a wonderful man, Gilbert," he said; "I can't understand you. You described yourself only this morning as being a nervous wreck—"

"Did I say that?" asked the other dryly.

"Well, you didn't admit it," said Leslie, with an aggrieved air, "but it was a description which most obviously fitted you. And yet in the face of this storm, which I confess curled me up pretty considerably, you take the seat of your chauffeur and you push the car through it. Moreover, you are sufficiently collected to pick up an old man when you had every excuse to leave him to his dismal fate."

For a moment Gilbert made no reply; then he laughed a little bitterly.

"There are a dozen ways of being nervous," he said, "and that doesn't happen to be one of mine. The old man is an important factor in my life, though he does not know it—the very instrument of fate."

He dropped his voice almost solemnly. Then he seemed to remember that the curious gaze of the other was upon him.

"I don't know where you got the impression that I was a nervous wreck," he said briefly. "It's hardly the ideal condition for a man who is to be married this week."

"That may be the cause, my dear chap," said the other reflectively. "I know a lot of people who are monstrously upset at the prospect. There was Tuppy Jones who absolutely ran away—lost his memory, or some such newspaper trick."

Gilbert smiled.

"I did the next worst thing to running away," he said a little moodily. "I wanted the wedding postponed."

"But why?" demanded the other. "I was going to ask you that this morning coming down, only it slipped my memory. Mrs. Cathcart told me she wouldn't hear of it."

Gilbert gave him no encouragement to continue the subject, but the voluble young man went on:

"Take what the gods give you, my son," he said. "Here you are with a Foreign Office appointment, an Under-Secretaryship looming in the near future, a most charming and beautiful bride in prospect, rich—"

"I wish you wouldn't say that," said Gilbert sharply. "The idea is abroad all over London. Beyond my pay I have no money whatever. This car," he said, as he saw the other's questioning face, "is certainly mine—at least, it was a present from my uncle, and I don't suppose he'll want it returned before I sell it. Thank God it makes no difference to you," he went on with that note of hardness still in his voice, "but I am half inclined to think that two-thirds of the friendships I have, and all the kindness which is from time to time shown to me, is based upon that delusion of riches. People think that I am my uncle's heir."

"But aren't you?" gasped the other. Gilbert shook his head.

"My uncle has recently expressed his intention of leaving the whole of his fortune to that admirable institution which is rendering such excellent service to the canine world—the Battersea Dogs' Home."

Leslie Frankfort's jovial face bore an expression of tragic bewilderment.

"Have you told Mrs. Cathcart this?" he asked.

"Mrs. Cathcart!" replied the other in surprise.

"No, 1 haven't told her. I don't think it's necessary. After all," he said with a smile, "Edith isn't marrying me for money, she is pretty rich herself, isn't she? Not that it matters," he said hastily, "whether she's rich or whether she's poor."

Neither of the two men spoke again for the rest of the journey, and at the corner of St. James's Street Gilbert put his friend down. He continued his way to the little house which he had taken furnished a year before, when marriage had only seemed the remotest of possibilities when his worldly prospects had seemed much brighter than they were at present.

Gilbert Standerton was a member of one of those peculiar families which seem to be made up entirely of nephews. His uncle, the eccentric old Anglo-Indian, had charged himself with the boy's future, and he had been mainly responsible for securing the post which Gilbert now held. More than this, he had made him his heir, and since he was a man who did, nothing in secret, and was rather inclined to garrulity, the news of Gilbert's good fortune was spread from one end of England to the other.

Then, a month before this story opens, had come like a bombshell a curt notification from his relative that he had deemed it advisable to alter the terms of his will, and that Gilbert might look for no more than the thousand pounds to which, in common with innumerable other nephews, he was entitled.

It was not a shock to Gilbert except that he was a little grieved with the fear that in some manner he had offended his fiery uncle. He had a too lively appreciation of the old man's goodness to him to resent the eccentricity which would make him a comparatively poor man.

It would have considerably altered the course of his life if he had notified at least one person of the change in his prospects.

III

Gilbert Leaves Hurriedly

G ilbert was dressing for dinner when the storm came up over London. It had lost none of its intensity or strength. For an hour the street had glared fitfully in the blue lightning of the electrical discharges, and the house rocked with crash after crash of thunder.

He himself was in tune with the elements, for there raged in his heart such a storm as shook the very foundations of his life. Outwardly there was no sign of distress. The face he saw in the shaving-glass was a mask, immobile and expressionless.

He sent his man to call a taxi-cab. The storm had passed over London, and only the low grumble of thunder could be heard when he came out on to the rain-washed streets. A few wind-torn wisps of cloud were hurrying at a great rate across the sky, stragglers endeavouring in frantic haste to catch up the main body.

He descended from his cab at the door of No. 274 Portland Square slowly and reluctantly. He had an unpleasant task to perform, as unpleasant to him, more unpleasant, indeed, than it could be to his future mother-in-law. He did not doubt that the suspicion implanted in his mind by Leslie was unfair and unworthy. He was ushered into the drawing-room, and found himself the solitary occupant. He looked at his watch.

"Am I very early, Cole?" he asked the butler.

"You are rather, sir," said the man, "but I will tell Miss Cathcart you are here."

Gilbert nodded. He strolled across to the window, and stood, his hands clasped behind him, looking out upon the wet street. He stood thus for five minutes, his head sunk forward on his breast, absorbed in thought. The opening of the door aroused him, and he turned to meet the girl who had entered.

Edith Cathcart was one of the most beautiful women in London, though "woman" might be too serious a word to apply to this slender girl who had barely emerged from her schooldays. In some grey eyes of a peculiar softness a furtive apprehension always seems to wait—a fear and an appeal at one and the same time. So it was with Edith

Cathcart. Those eyes of hers were for ever on guard, and even as they attracted they held the over-eager seeker of friendship at arm's length. The nose was just a little *retroussé;* the sensitive lips played supporter to the apprehensive eyes. She wore her hair low over her forehead; it was dark almost to a point of blackness. She was dressed in a plain gown of sea-green satin, with scarcely any jewel or ornamentation.

He walked to meet her with quick steps and took both her hands in his; his hungry eyes searched her face eagerly.

"You look lovely to-night, Edith," he said, in a voice scarcely above a whisper.

She released her hands gently with the ghost of a smile that subtly atoned for her action.

"Did you enjoy your Derby Day?" she asked.

"It was enormously interesting," he said; "it is extraordinary that I have never been before."

"You could not have chosen a worse day. Did you get caught in the storm? We have had a terrible one here."

She spoke quickly, with a little note of query at the end of each sentence. She gave you the impression that she desired to stand well with her lover, that she was in some awe of him. She was like a child, anxious to acquit herself well of a lesson; and now and then she conveyed a sense of relief, as one who had surmounted yet another obstacle.

Gilbert was always conscious of the strain which marked their relationship. A dozen times a day he told himself that it was incredible that such a strain should exist. But he found a ready excuse for her diffidence and the furtive fear which came and went in her eyes like shadows over the sea. She was young, much younger than her years. This beautiful bud had not opened yet, and his engagement had been cursed by over-much formality. He had met her conventionally at a ball. He had been introduced by her mother, again conventionally; he had danced with her and sat out with her; punted her on the river; motored her and her mother to Ascot. It was all very ordinary and commonplace. It lacked something. Gilbert never had any doubts as to that.

He took the blame upon himself for all deficiencies, though he was something of a romancist, despite the chilly formalism of the engagement. She had kept him in his place with the rest of the world, one arm's length, with those beseeching eyes of hers. He was at arm's-length when he proposed, in a speech the fluency of which was eloquent of the absence of, anything which touched emotionalism. And she had accepted in a murmured word, and turned a cold cheek for his kiss, and then had fluttered out of his arms like an imprisoned bird seeking its liberty, and had escaped from that conventional conservatory with its horrible palms and its spurious Tanagra statuettes.

Gilbert in love was something of a boy: an idealist, a dreamer. Other grown men have shared his weakness; there are unsuspected wells of romance in the most practical of men. So he was content with his dreams, weaving this and that story of sweet surrender in his inmost heart. He loved her, completely, absorbingly. To him she was a divine and a fragrant thing.

He had taken her hand again in his, and realized with pain, which was tinctured with amusement that made it bearable, that she was seeking to disengage herself, when Mrs. Cathcart came into the room.

She was a tall woman, still beautiful, though age had given her a certain angularity. The ravages of time had made it necessary for her to seek artificial aid for the strengthening of her attractions. Her mouth was thin, straight and uncompromising; her chin was too bony to be beautiful. She smiled as she rustled across the room and offered her gloved hand to the young man.

"You're early, Gilbert," she said.

"Yes," he replied awkwardly. Here was the opportunity which he sought, yet he experienced some reluctance in availing himself of the chance.

He had released the girl as the door opened, and she had instinctively taken a step backwards, and stood with her hands behind her, regarding him gravely and intently.

"Really," he said, "I wanted to see you."

"To see me?" asked Mrs. Cathcart archly. "No, surely not me!"

Her smile comprehended the girl and the young man. For some reason which he could not appreciate at the moment Gilbert felt uncomfortable.

"Yes, it was to see you," he said, "but it isn't remarkable at this particular period of time."

He smiled again.

She held up a warning finger.

"You must not bother about any of the arrangements. I want you to leave that entirely to me. You will find you have no cause to complain."

"Oh, it wasn't that," he said hastily; "it was something more—more—"

He hesitated. He wanted to convey to her the gravity of the business he had in hand. And even as he approached the question of an interview, a dim realization came to him of the difficulty of his position. How could he suggest to this woman, who had been all kindness and all sweetness to him, that he suspected her of motives which did credit neither to her head nor her heart? How could he broach the subject of his poverty to one who had not once but a hundred times confided to him that his expectations and the question of his future wealth were the only drawbacks to what she had described as an ideal love marriage?

"I almost wish you were poor, Gilbert," she had said. "I think riches are an awful handicap to young people circumstanced as you and Edith will be." She had conveyed this suspicion of his wealth more than once. And yet, at a chance word from Leslie, he had doubted the purity of her motives! He remembered with a growing irritation that it had been Mrs. Cathcart who had made the marriage possible; the vulgar-minded might even have gone further and suggested that she had thrown Edith at his head. There was plenty of groundwork for Leslie's suspicion, he thought, as he looked at the tall, stylish woman before him. Only he felt ashamed that he had listened to the insidious suggestion.

"Could you give me a quarter of an hour—"

He stopped. He was going to say "before dinner," but thought that possibly an interview after the meal would be less liable to interruption "—after dinner?"

"With pleasure," she smiled. "What are you going to do? Confess some of the irregularities of your youth?"

He shook his head with a little grimace.

"You may be sure I shall never tell you those," he said.

"Then I will see you after dinner," she assented. "There are a lot of people coming to-night, and I am simply up to my eyes in work. You bridegrooms," she patted his shoulder with her fan reproachfully, "have no idea what chaos you bring into the domestic life of your unfortunate relatives of the future."

Edith stood aloof, in the attitude she had adopted when he had released her, watchful, curious, in the scene, but not of it. It was an effect which the presence of Mrs. Cathcart invariably produced upon her daughter. It was not an obliteration, not exactly an eclipse, as the puzzled Gilbert had often observed. It was as though the entrance of one character of a drama were followed by the immediate exit of her who had previously occupied the scene. He pictured Edith waiting at the wings for a cue which would bring her into active existence again, and that cue was invariably the retirement of her mother.

"There are quite a number of nice people coming to-night, Gilbert," said Mrs. Cathcart, glancing at a slip of paper in her hand. "There are some you don't know, and some I want you very much to meet. I am sure you will like dear Dr. Cassylis—"

A smothered exclamation caught her ear, and she looked up sharply. Gilbert's face was set: it was void of all expression. The girl saw the mask and wondered.

"What is it?" asked Mrs. Cathcart.

"Nothing," said Gilbert steadily; "you were talking about your guests."

"I was saying that you must meet Dr. Barclay-Seymour—he is a most charming man. I don't think you know him?"

Gilbert shook his head.

"Well, you ought to," she said. "He's a dear friend of mine, and why on earth he practise in Leeds instead of maintaining an establishment in Harley Street I haven't the slightest idea. The ways of men are beyond finding out. Then there is. . ."

She reeled off a list of names, some of which Gilbert knew.

"What is the time?" she asked suddenly. Gilbert looked at his watch.

"A quarter to eight? I must go," she said. "I will see you immediately after dinner."

She turned back as she reached the door, irresolutely.

"I suppose you aren't going to change that absurd plan of yours," she asked hopefully. Gilbert had recovered his equanimity.

"I do not know to which absurd plan you are referring," he said.

"Spending your honeymoon in town," she replied.

"I don't think Gilbert should be bothered about that." It was the girl who spoke, her first intrusion into the conversation. Her mother glanced at her sharply.

"In this case, my dear," she said freezingly, "it is a matter in which I am more concerned than yourself."

Gilbert hastened to relieve the girl of the brunt of the storm. Mrs. Cathcart was not slow to anger, and although Gilbert himself had never felt the lash of her bitter tongue, he had a shrewd suspicion that his future wife had been a victim more than once.

"It is absolutely necessary that I should be in town on the days I referred to," he said. "I have asked you—"

"To postpone the wedding?" said Mrs. Cathcart. "My dear boy, I couldn't do that. It wasn't a reasonable request, now was it?" She smiled at him as sweetly as her inward annoyance allowed her.

"I suppose it wasn't," he said dubiously. He said no more, but waited until the door had closed behind her, then he turned quickly to the girl.

"Edith," he said, speaking rapidly, "I want you to do something for me."

"You want me to do something?" she asked in surprise.

"Yes, dearest. I must go away now. I want you to find some excuse to make to your mother. I've remembered a most important matter which I have not seen to—" He spoke hesitatingly, for he was no ready liar.

"Going away!" It was surprise rather than disappointment, he noticed, and was pardonably irritated.

"You can't go now," she said, and that look of fear came into her eyes. "Mother would be so angry. The people are arriving."

From where he stood he had seen three motor-broughams draw up almost simultaneously in front of the house.

"I must go," he said desperately. "Can't you get me out in any way? I don't want to meet these people; I've very good reasons."

She hesitated a moment.

"Where are your hat and coat?" she asked.

"In the hall—you will just have time," he said.

She was in the hall and back again with his coat, led him to the farther end of the drawing-room, through a door which communicated with the small library beyond. There was a way here to the garage and to the mews at the back of the house. She watched the tall, striding figure with a troubled gaze, then as he disappeared from view she fastened the library door and came back to the drawing-room in time to meet her mother.

"Where is Gilbert?" asked Mrs. Cathcart.

"Gone," said the girl.

"Gone!" Edith nodded slowly.

"He remembered something very important and had to go back to his house."

"But of course he is returning?"

"I don't think so, mother," she said quietly. "I fancy that the 'something' is immensely pressing."

"But this is nonsense!" Mrs. Cathcart stamped her foot. "Here are all the people whom I have specially invited to meet him. It's disgraceful!"

"But, mother—"

"Don't 'but mother' me, for God's sake!" said Mrs. Cathcart.

They were alone, the guests were assembling in the larger drawing-room, and there was no need for the elder woman to disguise her feelings. "You sent him away, I suppose?" she said.

"I don't blame him. How can you expect to keep a man at your side if you treat him as though he were a grocer calling for orders?"

The girl listened wearily, and did not raise her eyes from the carpet.

"I do my best," she said in a low voice.

"Your worst must be pretty bad if that is your best. After I've strained my every effort to bring to you one of the richest young men in London you might, at least, pretend that his presence is welcome; but if he were the devil himself you couldn't show greater reluctance at meeting him or greater relief at his departure."

"Mother!" said the girl, and her eyes were filled with tears.

"Don't 'mother' me, please!" said Mrs. Cathcart, deliberately.

"I am sick to death of your faddiness and your prejudices. What on earth do you want? What am I to get you?" She threw out her arms in exasperated despair.

"I don't want to marry at all," said the girl in a low voice. "My father would never have forced me to marry."

It was a daring thing to say, an exhibition of greater boldness than she had ever shown before in her encounters with her mother. But lately there had come to her a new courage. That despair which made her dumb glowed now to rage, the fires of rebellion smouldered in her heart; and, albeit the demonstrations of her growing resentment were few and far between, her courage grew upon her venturing.

"Your father!" breathed Mrs. Cathcart, white with rage; "am I to have your father thrown at my head? Your father was a fool! A fool!" She almost hissed the word. "He ruined me as he ruined you because he hadn't sufficient sense to keep the money he had inherited. I thought he was a clever man. I looked up to him for twenty years as the embodiment of all that was wise and kind and genial, and all those twenty years he was frittering away his competence on every hare-brained scheme which the needy adventurers of finance brought to him. He would not have forced you! I swear he wouldn't!"

She laughed bitterly.

"He would have married you to the chauffeur if your heart was that way inclined. He was all amiability and incompetence, all good nature and inefficiency. I hate your father!" Her blue eyes were opened to their widest extent and the cold glare of hate was indeed apparent to the shrinking girl.

"I hate him every time I have to entertain a shady stockbroker for the advantage I may receive from his knowledge of the market; I hate him for every economy I have to practise; I hate him every time I see my meagre dividends come in, and as I watch them swallowed up by the results of his folly. Don't make me hate you," she said, pointing a warning finger at the girl.

Edith had cowered before the torrent of words, but this slander of her dead father roused something within her, put aside all fear of consequence, even though that consequence might be a further demonstration of that anger which she so dreaded. Now she stood erect, facing the woman she called mother, her face pale, but her chin tilted a little defiantly.

"You may say what you like about me, mother," she said quietly, "but I will not have you defame my father. I have done all you requested: I am going to marry a man who, though I know he is a kindly and charming man, is no more to me than the first individual I might meet in the street to-night. I am making this sacrifice for your sake: do not ask me to forego my faith in the man who is the one lovable memory in my life."

Her voice broke a little, her eyes were bright with tears.

Whatever Mrs. Cathcart might have said, and there were many things she could have said, was checked by the entry of a servant. For a moment or two they stood facing one another, mother and daughter, in silence. Then without another word Mrs. Cathcart turned on her heel and walked out of the room.

The girl waited for a moment, then went back to the library through which Gilbert had passed. She closed the door behind her and turned on one of the lights, for it was growing dark. She was shaking from head to foot with the play of these pent emotions of hers. She could have wept, but with anger and shame. For the first time in her life her mother had shown her heart. The concentrated bitterness of years had poured forth, unchecked by pity or policy. She had revealed the hate which for all these years had been gnawing at her soul; revealed in a flash the relationship between her father and her mother which the girl had never suspected.

That they had not been on the most affectionate terms Edith knew, but her short association with the world in which they moved had reconciled her mind to the coolness which characterized the attitudes of husband and wife. She had seen a score of such houses where man and wife were on little more than friendly terms, and had accepted such conditions as normal. It aroused in her a wild irritation that such relationships should exist: child as she was, she had felt that something was missing. But it had also reconciled her to her marriage with Gilbert Standerton. Her life with him would be no worse, and probably might be a little better, than the married lives of those people with whom she was brought into daily contact.

But in her mother's vehemence she caught a glimpse of the missing quality of marriage. She knew now why her gentle father had changed suddenly from a genial, kindly man, with his quick laugh and his too willing ear for the plausible, into a silent shadow of a man, the sad broken figure she so vividly retained in her memory.

Here was a quick turn in the road of life for her, an unexpected vista flashing into view suddenly before her eyes. It calmed her, steadied her. In those few minutes of reflection, standing there in the commonplace, gloomy little library, watching through the latticed panes the dismal mews which offered itself for inspection through a parallelogram of bricked courtyard, she experienced one of those great and subtle changes which come to humanity.

There was a new outlook, a new standard by which to measure her fellows, a new philosophy evolved in the space of a second. It was a tremendous upheaval of settled conviction which this tiny apartment witnessed.

She was surprised herself at the calmness with which she returned to the drawing-room and joined the party now beginning to assemble. It came as a shock to discover that she was examining her mother with the calm, impartial scrutiny of one who was not in any way associated with her. Mrs. Cathcart observed the girl's self-possession and felt a twinge of uneasiness. She addressed her unexpectedly, hoping to surprise her to embarrassment, and was a little staggered by the readiness with which the girl met her gaze and the coolness with which she disagreed to some proposition which the elder woman had made.

It was a new experience to the masterful Mrs. Cathcart. The girl might be sulking, but this was a new variety of sulks, foreign to Mrs. Cathcart's experience.

She might be angry, yet there was no sign of anger; hurt—she should have been in tears. Mrs. Cathcart's experienced eye could detect no sign of weeping. She was puzzled, a little alarmed. She had gone too far, she thought, and must conciliate, rather than carry on the feud until the other sued for forgiveness.

It irritated her to find herself in this position; but she was a tactician first and foremost, and it would be bad tactics on her part to pursue a disadvantage. Rather she sought the *status quo ante bellum,* and was annoyed to discover that it had gone for ever.

She hoped the talk that evening would confuse the girl to the point of seeking her protection; but to her astonishment Edith spoke of her marriage as she had never spoken of it before, without embarrassment, without hesitation, coolly, reasonably, intelligently.

The end of the evening found Edith commanding her field and her mother in the position of a suitor.

Mrs. Cathcart waited till the last guest had gone, then she came into the smaller drawing-room to find Edith standing in the fireplace, looking thoughtfully at a paper which lay upon the mantelshelf.

"What is it interests you so much, dear?"

The girl looked round, picked up the paper and folded it slowly.

"Nothing particularly," she said. "Your Dr. Cassylis is an amusing man."

"He is a very clever man," said her mother, tartly. She had infinite faith in doctors, and offered them the tribute which is usually reserved for the supernatural.

"Is he?" said the girl coolly. "I suppose he is. Why does he live in Leeds?"

"Really, Edith, you are coming out of your shell," said her mother with a forced smile of admiration. "I have never known you take so much interest in the people of the world before."

"I am going to take a great deal of interest in people," said the girl steadily. "I have been missing so much all my life."

"I think you are being a little horrid," said her mother, repressing her anger with an effort; "you're certainly being very unkind. I suppose all this nonsense has arisen out of my mistaken confidence."

The girl made no reply.

"I think I'll go to bed, mother," she said.

"And whilst you're engaged in settling your estimate of people," said Mrs. Cathcart with ominous calm, "perhaps you will interpret your fiance's behaviour to me. Dr. Cassylis particularly wanted to meet him."

"I am not going to interpret anything," said the girl.

"Don't employ that tone with me," replied her mother, sharply.

The girl stopped, she was half-way to the door. She hardly turned, but spoke to her mother over her shoulder.

"Mother," she said, quietly but decidedly, "I want you to understand this: if there is any more bother, or if I am again made the victim of your crossness, I shall write to Gilbert and break off my engagement."

"Are you mad?" gasped the woman. Edith shook her head.

"No, I am tired," she said; "tired of many things."

There was much that Mrs. Cathcart could have said, but with a belated wisdom she held her tongue till the door had closed behind her daughter. Then, late as the hour was, she sent for the cook and settled herself grimly for a pleasing half hour, for the *vol-au-vent* had been atrocious.

IV

The Melody in F

G ilbert Standerton was dressing slowly before his glass when Leslie was announced. That individual was radiant and beautiful to behold, as became the best man at the wedding of an old friend.

Leslie Frankfort was one of those fortunate individuals who combine congenial work with the enjoyment of a private income. He was the junior partner of a firm of big stockbrokers in the City, a firm which dealt only with the gilt-edged markets of finance. He enjoyed in common with Gilbert a taste for classical music, and this was the bond which had first drawn the two men together. He came into the room, deposited his silk hat carefully upon a chair, and sat on the edge of the bed, offering critical suggestions to the prospective bridegroom.

"By the way," he said suddenly, "I saw that old man of yours yesterday."

Gilbert looked round.

"You mean Springs, the musician?" The other nodded.

"He was playing for the amusement of a theatre queue—a fine old chap."

"Very," said Gilbert absently. He paused in his dressing, took up a letter from the table, and handed it to the other.

"Am I to read it?" asked Leslie.

Gilbert nodded.

"There's nothing to read, as a matter of fact," he said; "it's my uncle's wedding present."

The young man opened the envelope and extracted the pink slip. He looked at the amount and whistled.

"One hundred pounds," he said. "Good Lord! that won't pay the upkeep of your car for a quarter. I suppose you told Mrs. Cathcart?"

Gilbert shook his head.

"No," he said shortly; "I intended telling her but I haven't. I am perfectly satisfied in my own mind, Leslie, that we are doing her an injustice. She has been so emphatic about money. And after all, I'm not a pauper," he said with a smile.

"You're worse than a pauper," said Leslie earnestly; "a man with six hundred a year is the worst kind of pauper I know."

"Why?"

"You'll never bring your tastes below a couple of thousand, you'll never raise your income above six hundred—plus your Foreign Office job, that's only another six hundred."

"Work," said the other.

"Work!" said the other scornfully; "you don't earn money by work. You earn money by scheming, by getting the better of the other fellow. You're too soft-hearted to make money, my son."

"You seem to make money," said Gilbert with a little smile.

Leslie shook his head vigorously.

"I've never made a penny in my life," he confessed with some enjoyment. "No, I have got some very stout, unimaginative senior partners who do all the money-making. I merely take dividends at various periods of the year. But then I was in luck. What is your money, by the way?"

Gilbert was in the act of tying his cravat. He looked up with a little frown.

"What do you mean?" he asked.

"I mean, is it in securities—does it continue after your death?"

The little frown still knit the brows of the other.

"No," he said shortly; "after my death there is scarcely enough to bring in a hundred and fifty a year. I am only enjoying a life on this particular property."

Leslie whistled.

"Well, I hope, old son, that you're well insured." The other man made no attempt to interrupt as Leslie arguing with great fluency and skill on the duties and responsibilities of heads of families, delivered himself of his views on insurance and upon the uninsured.

"Some Johnnies are so improvident," he said. "I knew a man—"

He stopped suddenly. He had caught a reflection of Gilbert's face in the glass. It was haggard and drawn, it seemed the face of a man in mortal agony. Leslie sprang up.

"What on earth is the matter, my dear chap?" he cried. He came to the other's side and laid his hand on his shoulder.

"Oh, it's nothing—nothing, Leslie," said Gilbert. He passed his hand before his eyes as though to wipe away some ugly vision.

"I'm afraid I've been rather a careless devil. You see, I depended too much upon uncle's money. I ought to be insured."

"That isn't worrying you surely?" asked the other in astonishment.

"It worries me a bit," said Gilbert moodily. "One never knows, you know—"

He stood looking thoughtfully at the other his hands thrust into his pockets.

"I wish to heaven this wedding had been postponed!"

Leslie laughed.

"It's about time you were married," he said. "What a jumpy ass you are."

He looked at his watch.

"You'd better hurry up, or you'll be losing this bride of yours. After all, this isn't a day for gloom, it's the day of days, my friend."

He saw the soft look that came into Gilbert's eyes, and felt satisfied with his work.

"Yes, there is that," said Gilbert Standerton softly. "I forgot all my blessings. God bless her!" he said under his breath.

As they were leaving the house, Gilbert asked: "I suppose you have a list of the guests who are to he present?"

"Yes," said the other, "Mrs. Cathcart was most duteous."

"Will Dr. Barclay-Seymour be there?" asked the other carelessly.

"Barclay-Seymour—no, he won't be there," replied Leslie, "he's the Leeds Johnnie, isn't he? He went up from London last night. What's this talk of your having run away the other night?"

"It was an important engagement," said Gilbert hurriedly, "I had a man to see; I couldn't very well put him off—"

Leslie realized that he had asked an embarrassing question and changed the subject. "By the way," he said, "I shouldn't mention this matter of the money to Mrs. Cathcart till after you've both settled down."

"I won't," said Gilbert grimly.

On the way to the church he reviewed all the troubles that were besetting him and faced them squarely. Perhaps it would not be as bad as he thought. He was ever prone to take an exaggerated and a worrying view of troubles. He had anticipated dangers, and time and time again his fears had been groundless. He had lived too long alone. A man ought to be married before he was thirty-two. That was his age. He had become cranky. He found consolation in uncomplimentary analysis till the church was reached.

It was a dream, that ceremony: the crowded pews, the organ, the white-robed choir, the rector and his assistants; the coming of Edith, so beautiful, so ethereal in her bridal robes; the responses, the kneeling and the rising—it was all unreal.

He had thought that the music would have made a lasting impression on him; he had been at some pains to choose it, and had had several consultations with the organist. But at the end of the service, when he began to walk, still in his dream, towards the vestry, he could not recall one single bar. He had a dim recollection of the fact that above the altar was a stained glass window, one tiny pane of which had been removed, evidently on account of a breakage.

He was back in the house, sitting at the be-flowered table, listening in some confusion to the speeches and the bursts of laughter which assailed each speaker as he made his point: now he was on his feet, talking easily, without effort, but what words he used, or why people applauded, or why they smiled he could not say. Once in its course he had looked down at the delicate face by his side, and had met those solemn eyes of hers, less fearful to-day, it seemed, than ever he had seen them. He had felt for her hand and had held it, cold and unresponsive, in his. . .

"An excellent speech," said Leslie.

They were in the drawing-room after the breakfast.

"You're quite an orator."

"Am I?" said Gilbert. He was beginning to wake again. The drawing-room was real, these people were real, the jokes, the badinage, and the wit which flew from tongue to tongue—all these things were of a life he knew.

"Whew!" He wiped his forehead and breathed a deep sigh. He felt like a man who had regained consciousness after an anaesthetic that did not quite take effect. A painless and a beautiful experience, but of another world, and it was not he, so he told himself, who had knelt at the altar rail.

OFFICIALLY THE HONEYMOON WAS TO be spent at Harrogate, actually it was to be spent in London. They preserved the pretence of catching a train, and drove to King's Cross.

No word was spoken throughout that journey. Gilbert felt the restriction, and did not challenge it or seek to overcome it. The girl was naturally silent. She had so much to say in the proper place and at the proper time. He saw the old fear come back to her eyes, was hurt by the unconscious and involuntary shrinking when his hand touched hers.

The carriage was dismissed at King's Cross. A taxi-cab was engaged, and they drove to the house in St. John's Wood. It was empty, the servants had been sent away on a holiday, but it was a perfectly fitted little mansion. There were electric cookers, and every labour-saving appliance the mind of man could devise, or a young man with great expectations and no particular idea of the value of money could acquire.

This was to be one of the joys of the honeymoon, so Gilbert had told himself. She had willingly dispensed with her maid; he was ready to be man-of-all-work, to cook and to serve, leaving the rough work for the two new day servants he had employed to come in in the morning.

Yet it was with no sense of joyfulness that he led her from room to room, showed her the treasures of his household. A sense of apprehension of some coming trouble laid its hand upon his tongue, damped his spirit, and held him in temporary bondage.

The girl was self-possessed. She admired, criticized kindly, and rallied him gently upon his domesticity. But the strain was there all the time; there was a shadow which lay between them.

She went to her room to change. They had arranged to go out to dinner, and this programme they followed. Leslie Frankfort saw them in the dining hall of Princes, and pretended he didn't know them. It was ten o'clock when they went back to their little house.

Gilbert went to his study; his wife had gone up to her room and had promised to come down for coffee. He went to work with all the skill which a pupil of Rahbat might be expected to display, and brewed two tiny little cups of Mocha. This he served on the table near the settee where she would sit. . . Then she came in.

He had been fast awakening from the dream of the morning. He was alive now. The dazement of that momentous ceremony had worn away. He rose and went a little way towards her. He would have taken her in his arms then and there, but this time the arm's length was a reality. Her hand touched his breast, and the arm stiffened. He felt the rebuff in the act, and it seemed to him that his heart went cold, and that all the vague terrors of the previous days crystallized into one concrete and terrible truth. He knew all that she had to say before she spoke.

It was some time before she found the words she wanted, the opening was so difficult.

"Gilbert," she said at last, "I am going to do a cowardly thing. It is only cowardly because I have not told you before."

He motioned her to the settee. He had woven a little romance for this moment, a dream scene which was never to be enacted. Here was the shattering.

"I won't sit down," she said, "I want all my strength to tell you what I have to tell you. If I hadn't been an arrant coward I should have told you last night. I meant to tell you," she said, "but you did not come."

He nodded.

"I know," he said, almost impatiently.

"I could not come. I did not wish—I could not come," he repeated. "You know what I have to tell you?" Her eyes were steadily fixed on his. "Gilbert, I do not love you."

He nodded again.

"I know now," he said.

"I never have loved you," she said in tones of despair; "there never was any time when I regarded you as more than a dear friend. But—"

She wanted to tell him why, but a sense of loyalty to her mother kept her silent. She would take all the blame, for was she not blameworthy? For she, at least, was mistress of her own soul: had she wished, she could have taken a line of greater resistance than that which she had followed.

"I married you," she went on slowly, "because—because you are—rich—because you will be rich." Her voice dropped at the last word until it was husky. There was a hard fight going on within her.

She wanted to tell the truth, and yet she did not want. him to think so badly of her as that.

"For my money!" he repeated wonderingly.

"Yes, I—I wanted to marry a man with money. We have had—a very hard time."

The confession came in little gasps; she had to frame every sentence before she spoke.

"You mustn't blame mother, I was equally guilty; and I ought to have told you—I wanted to tell you."

"I see," he said calmly.

It is wonderful what reserves of strength come at a man's bidding. In this terrible crisis, in this moment when the whole of his life's happiness was shattered, when the fabric of his dream was crumbling like a house of paper he could be judicial, almost phlegmatic.

He saw her sway, and springing to her side caught her.

"Sit down," he said quietly.

She obeyed without protest. He settled her in the corner of the settee, pushed a cushion almost viciously behind her, and walked back to the fireplace.

"So you married me for my money," he said, and laughed.

It was not without its amusing side, this situation.

"By heaven, what a comedy—what a comedy!" He laughed again. "My poor child," he said, with unaccustomed irony, "I am sorry for you, for you have secured neither husband nor money!"

She looked up at him quickly.

"Nor money," she repeated.

There was only interest that he saw in her eyes. There was no hint of disappointment. He knew the truth, more than she had told him: it was not she who desired a fortune, it was this mother of hers, this domineering, worldly woman.

"No husband and no money," he repeated savagely, in spite of the almost yearning desire which was in him to spare her. "And worse than that"—with two rapid strides he was at the desk which separated them, and bent across it, leaning heavily—"not only have you no husband, and not only is there no money, but—"

He stopped as if he had been shot.

The girl, looking at him, saw his face go drawn and grey, saw the eyes starting wildly past her, the mouth open in tragic dismay. She got up quickly.

"What is it? What is it?" she whispered in alarm.

"My God!"

His voice was cracked; it was the voice of a man in terror. She half bent her head, listening. From somewhere beneath the window arose the soft, melancholy strains of a violin. The music rose and fell, sobbing and pulsating with passion beneath the magic of the player's fingers. She stepped to a window and looked out. On the edge of the pavement a girl was playing, a girl whose poverty of dress did not hide her singular beauty.

The light from the street lamp fell upon her pale face, her eyes were fixed on the window where Gilbert was standing. Edith looked at her husband. He was shaking like a man with fever.

"The 'Melody in F,'" he whispered. "My God! The 'Melody in F'—and on my wedding day!"

V

The Man Who Desired Wealth

Leslie Frankfort was one of a group of three who stood in the inner office of Messrs. Warrell & Bird before a huge safe. There was plenty to attract and hold their attention, for the floor was littered with tools of every shape and description.

The safe itself bore evidence of a determined assault. A semi-circle of holes had been burnt in its solid iron door about the lock.

"They did that with an oxyhydrogen blow-pipe," said one of the men.

He indicated a number of iron tubes which lay upon the ground with the rest of the paraphernalia. "They made a thorough job of it. I wonder what disturbed them."

The eldest of the men shook his head.

"I expect the night watchman may have alarmed them," he said. "What do you think, Frankfort?"

"I haven't got over my admiration for their thoroughness yet," said Leslie. "Why the beggars must have used about a couple of hundred pounds' worth of tools."

He pointed to the kit on the ground. The detective's gaze followed his extended finger.

He smiled.

"Yes," he said quietly, "these people are pretty thorough. You say you've lost nothing?"

Mr. Warrell shook his head.

"Yes and no," he said carefully. "There was a diamond necklace which was deposited there last week by a client of ours—that has gone. I am anxious for the moment that this loss should not be reported."

The detective looked at him wonderingly.

"That is rather a curious request," he said, with a smile; "and you don't usually have diamond necklaces in a stockbroker's office—if I may be allowed to make that critical remark."

Mr. Warrell smiled.

"It isn't usual," he said, "but a client of ours who went abroad last week came in just twenty minutes before the train left, and asked us to take care of the jewel cases."

Mr. Warrell said this carelessly. He did not explain to the detective that they were held as security against the very large difference which the client had incurred; nor did he think it necessary to explain that he had kept the jewels in the office in the hope that the embarrassed lady might be able to redeem them.

"Did anybody know they were there except yourself and your partners?"

Warrell shook his head. "I don't think so. I have never mentioned it to anybody. Have you, Leslie?"

Leslie hesitated.

"Well, I'm bound to admit that I did," he confessed, "though it was to somebody who would not repeat it."

"Who was it?" asked Warrell.

"To Gilbert Standerton. I certainly mentioned the matter when we were discussing safe robberies."

The elder man nodded,

"I hardly think he is the sort of person who is likely to burgle a safe."

He smiled.

"It is a very curious coincidence," said Leslie reflectively, "that he and I were talking about this very gang only a couple of days ago, before he was married. I suppose," he asked the detective suddenly, "there is no doubt that this is the work of your international friend?"

Chief Inspector Goldberg nodded his head.

"No doubt whatever, sir," he said. "There is only one gang in England which could do this, and I could lay my hands on them to-day, but it would be a million pounds to one against my being able to secure at the same time evidence to convict them."

Leslie nodded brightly.

"That is what I was telling Gilbert," he said, turning to his partner. "Isn't it extraordinary that these things can be in the twentieth century? Here we have three or four men who are known—you told me their names, Inspector, after the last attempt—and yet the police are powerless to bring home their guilt to them. It does seem curious, doesn't it?"

Inspector Goldberg was not amused, but he permitted himself to smile politely.

"But then you've got to remember how difficult it is to collect evidence against men who work on such a huge scale as do these bank smashers. What I can't understand," he said, "is what attraction your safe has for them. This second attempt is a much more formidable one than the last."

"Yes, this is really a burglary," said Mr. Warrell. "In the last case there was nothing so elaborate in their preparations, though they were much more successful, in so far as they were able to open the safe."

"I suppose you don't want more of this to get in the papers than you can help," said the Inspector.

Mr. Warrell shook his head. "I don't want any of it to get in till I have seen my client," he said; "but I am entirely in your hands, and you must make such arrangements as you deem necessary."

"Very good," said the detective. "For the moment I do not think it is necessary to make any statement at all. If the reporters get hold of it, you had better tell them as much of the truth as you want to tell them, but the chances are that they won't even get to hear of it as you communicated directly to the Yard."

The police officer spent half an hour collecting and making notes of such data as he was able to secure. At the end of that time the Old Jewry sent a contingent of plain clothes policemen to remove the tools.

The burglars had evidently entered the office after closing hours on the previous night, and had worked through the greater part of the evening, and possibly far into the night, in their successful attempt to cut out the lock of the safe. That they had been disturbed in their work was evident from the presence of the tools. This was not their first burglary in the City of London. During the previous six months the City had been startled by a succession of daring robberies, the majority of which had been successful.

The men had shown extraordinary knowledge of the safe's contents, and it was this fact which had induced the police to narrow their circle of inquiry to three apparently innocent members of an outside broker's firm. But try as they might, no evidence could be secured which might even remotely associate them with the crime. Leslie remembered now that he had laughingly challenged Gilbert Standerton to qualify for the big reward which two firms at least had offered for the recovery of their stolen goods.

"After all," he said, "with your taste and genius, you would make an ideal thief-catcher."

"Or a thief," Gilbert had answered moodily. It had been one of his bad days, a day on which his altered prospects had preyed upon him.

A telegram was waiting for Leslie when he entered the narrow portals of the City Proscenium Club. He took it down and opened it leisurely, and read its contents. A puzzled frown gathered on his forehead. It ran:

I Must See You This Afternoon. Meet Me at Charing Cross Station Four O'clock.

Gilbert

Punctually to the minute Leslie reached the terminus. He found Gilbert pacing to and fro beneath the clock, and was shocked at his appearance.

"What on earth is the matter with you?" he asked.

"Matter with me?" demanded the other hardly; "what do you think is the matter with me?"

"Are you in trouble?" asked Leslie anxiously. He was genuinely fond of this friend of his.

"Trouble?" Gilbert laughed bitterly. "My dear good chap, I am always in trouble. Haven't I been in trouble since the first day I met you? I want you to do something for me," he went on briskly. "You were talking the other day about money. I have recognized the tragedy of my own dependence. I have got to get money, and get it quick."

He spoke briskly, and in a matter-of-fact tone, but Leslie heard a determination which had never formed part of his friend's equipment.

"I want to know something about shares and stocks and things of that sort," Gilbert went on, "You'll have to instruct me. I don't suppose you know much about it yourself"—he smiled, with a return to the old good-humour—"but what little you know you've got to impart to me."

"My dear chap," protested the other, "why the devil are you worrying about a thing like that on your honeymoon? Where is your wife, by the way?"

"Oh, she's at the house," said the other shortly. He did not feel inclined to discuss her, and Leslie, in his amazement, had sufficient tact to pass over the subject.

"I can tell you all I know now, if you want a tip," he said.

"I want something bigger than a tip—I want investments. I want you to tell me something that will bring in about twelve thousand a year."

Leslie stopped and looked at the other.

"Are you quite—?" he began.

Gilbert smiled, a crooked little smile.

"Am I right in my head?" he finished. "Oh, yes, I am quite sane."

"But don't you see," said the other, "you would want a little over a quarter of a million to bring in that interest."

Gilbert nodded.

"I had an idea that some such amount was required. I want you to get me out between to-night and to-morrow a list of securities in which I can invest and which must be gilt-edged, and must, as I say, secure for me, or for my heirs, the sum I have mentioned."

"And did you," asked the indignant Leslie, "bring me to this beastly place on a hot afternoon in June to pull my leg about your dream investments?" But something in Gilbert's face checked his humour. "Seriously, do you mean this?" he asked.

"Seriously, I mean it."

"Well, then, I'll give you the list like a shot. What has happened— has uncle relented?"

Gilbert shook his head.

"He is not likely to relent," he said. "As a matter of fact, I had a note to-day from his secretary to tell me that he is pretty ill. I'm awfully sorry." There was a genuine note of regret in his tone. "He is a decent old chap."

"There's no reason why he should hand over his wealth to the 'demnition bow-wows,'" quoted Leslie indignantly. "But why did you meet me here, my son? Your club is round the corner."

"I know," said Gilbert; "but the club is—well, to tell you the truth," he said, "I am giving up the club."

"Giving up your club?" He stood squarely before the taller man. "Now just tell me," he asked deliberately, "what the Dickens all this means? You're giving up your club, you'll be giving up your Foreign Office job next, my Croesus!"

Gilbert nodded.

"I have given up the Foreign Office work," he said quietly. "I want all the time I can get," he went on, speaking rapidly. "I want every moment of the day for my own plans and my own schemes. You don't know what it's all about, my dear chap"—he laid his hand affectionately on the other's shoulder—"but just believe that I am in urgent need of all the advice you can give me, and I only want the advice for which I ask."

"Which means that I am not to poke my nose in your business unless I have a special invitation card all printed and decorated. Very good," laughed Leslie. "Now come along to my club. I suppose as a result of your brief married life you haven't conceived a dislike to all clubs?"

Gilbert made no answer, nor did they return again to the subject until they were ensconced in the spacious smoking-room of the Junior Terriers.

For two hours the men sat there, Gilbert questioning eagerly, pointedly, jotting down notes upon a sheet of paper. The other answered, often with some difficulty, the running fire of questions which his friend put.

"I didn't know how little I knew," confessed the young man ruefully, as Gilbert wrote down the last answer to the very last question. "What an encyclopaedic questioner you are; you're a born examiner, Gilbert."

Gilbert smiled faintly as he slipped the sheet of paper into his pocket.

"By the way," he said, as they were leaving the club, "I made my will this morning and I want you to be my executor."

Leslie pushed his hat back with a groan.

"You're the most cheerless bird I've met for quite a long time," he said in exasperation. "You were married yesterday, you're wandering round to-day with a face as long as an undertaker's tout—I understand such interesting and picturesque individuals exist in the East End of London—you've chucked up the billet that's bringing you in quite a lot of money, you've discussed investments, and you've made your will. You're a most depressing devil!"

Again Gilbert smiled: he was grimly amused. He shook hands with the young man before the club and called a taxi-cab to him.

"I'm going to St. John's Wood. I suppose you're not going my way?"

"I am relieved to hear that you are going to St. John's Wood," said the other with mock politeness. "I feared you were going to the nearest crematorium."

Gilbert found his wife in the study on his return. She was sitting on the big settee reading. The stress of the previous night had left no mark upon her beautiful face. She favoured him with a smile. Instinctively they had both adopted the attitude which best met the circumstances. Her respect for him had increased, even in that short space of time; he had so well mastered himself in that moment of terror—terror which in an indefinable way had communicated itself to her. He had met her the next morning at breakfast cheerfully; but she did not doubt that he had spent a sleepless night, for his eyes were heavy and tired, and in spite of his geniality his voice was sharp, as are the voices of men who have cheated Nature.

He walked straight to his desk now.

"Do you want to be alone?" she asked. He looked up with a start.

"No, no," he said hastily; "I've no wish to be alone. I've a little work to do, but you won't bother me. You ought to know," he said with an affectation of carelessness, "that I am resigning my post."

"Your post!" she repeated.

"Yes; I find I have so much to do, and the Foreign Office takes up so much of my time that I really can't spare, that it came to a question of giving up that or something else."

He did not enlighten her as to what that "something else" was, nor could she guess. Already he was an enigma to her; she found, strange though it seemed to her, a new interest in him. That there was some tragedy in his life, a tragedy unsuspected by her, she did not doubt. He had told her calmly and categorically the story of his disinheritance; at his request, she had put the whole of that story into a letter which she had addressed to her mother. She felt no qualms, no inward quaking, at the prospect of the inevitable encounter, though Mrs. Cathcart would be enraged beyond reason.

Edith smiled a little to herself as she had stuck down the flap of the envelope. This was poetic justice, though she herself might be a life-long sufferer by reason of her worldly parent's schemings. She had hoped that as a result of that letter, posted early in the morning, her mother would have called and the interview would have been finished before her husband returned. But Gilbert had been in the house half an hour when the blow fell. The tinkle of the hall bell brought the girl to her feet: she had been waiting, her ears strained, for that aggressive ring.

She herself flew down the stairs to open the door.

Mrs. Cathcart entered without a word, and as the girl closed the door behind her she turned.

"Where is that precious husband of yours?" she asked in a choked voice.

"My husband is in his study," said the girl calmly. "Do you want him, mother?"

"Do I want him?" she repeated in a choked voice. Edith saw the glare in the woman's eyes, saw, too, the pinched and haggard cheek. For one brief moment she pitied this woman, who had seen all her dreams shattered at a moment when she had hoped that their realization was inevitable.

"Does he know I am coming?"

"I think he rather expects you," said the girl dryly.

"I will see him by myself," said Mrs. Cathcart, turning half-way up the stairs.

"You will see him with me, mother, or you will not see him at all," said the girl.

"You will do as I tell you, Edith," stormed the woman.

The girl smiled.

"Mother," she said gently, "you have ceased to have any right to direct me. You have handed me over to another guardian whose claims are greater than yours."

It was not a good preparation for the interview that was to follow. Edith recognized this even as she opened the door and ushered her mother in. When Gilbert saw who his visitor was he rose with a little bow. He did not offer his hand. He knew something of what this woman was feeling.

"Won't you sit down, Mrs. Cathcart?" he said.

"I'll stand for what I have to say," she snapped. "Now, what is the meaning of this?"

She threw down the letter which the girl had written, and which she had read and re-read until every word was engraved on her mind.

"Is it true," she asked fiercely, "that you are a poor man? That you have deceived us? That you have lied your way into a marriage—?"

He held up his hand.

"You seem to forget, Mrs. Cathcart," he said with dignity, "that the question of my position has already been discussed by you and me, and you have been most emphatic in impressing upon me the fact that no worldly considerations would weigh with you."

"Worldly!" she sneered. "What do you mean by worldly, Mr. Standerton? Are you not in the world? Do you not live in a house and eat bread and butter that costs money? Do you not use motor-cars that require money for their upkeep? Whilst I am living in the world and you are living in the world, worldly considerations will always count. I thought you were a rich man; you're a beggar."

He smiled a little contemptuously.

"A pretty mess you've made of it," she said harshly. "You've got a woman who doesn't love you—I suppose you know that?"

He bowed.

"I know all that, Mrs. Cathcart," he said. "I knew the worst when I learnt that. The fact that you so obviously planned the marriage because you thought that I was Sir John Standerton's heir does not hurt me, because I have met so many women like you, only"—he shrugged his shoulders—"I must confess that I thought you were a little different to the rest of worldly mothers—forgive me if I use that word again. But you are not any better—you may be a little worse," he said, his thoughtful eyes upon her face. He was looking at her with a curious something which the woman could not quite understand in his eyes. She had seen that look somewhere, and in spite of herself she shivered. The anger died away in fear.

"I wanted you to postpone this wedding," he went on softly. "I had an especial reason—a reason I will not give you, but which will interest you in a few months' time. But you were fearful of losing your rich son-in-law. I didn't realize then that that was your fear. I have satisfied myself—it really doesn't matter how," he said steadily, "that you are more responsible than I for this good match."

He was a changed man. Mrs. Cathcart in her gusty rage could recognize this: there was a new soul, a new spirit, a new determination, and—that was it!—a new and terrible ferocity which shone from his eyes and for the moment hardened his face till it was almost terrible to look upon.

"Your daughter married me under a misapprehension. She told you all that I had to tell—almost all," he corrected himself, "and I anticipated this visit. Had you not come I should have sent for you. Your daughter is as free as the air as far as I am concerned. I suppose your worldliness extends to a knowledge of the law? She can sue for a divorce to-morrow, and attain it without any difficulty and with little publicity."

A gleam of hope came to the woman's face.

"I never thought of that," she said, half to herself. She turned quickly to her daughter, for she was a woman of action.

"Get your things and come with me."

Edith did not stir. She stood the other side of the table, half facing her husband and wholly facing her mother.

"You hear what Mr. Standerton says," said Mrs. Cathcart irritably. "He has opened a way of escape to you. What he says is true. A divorce *can* be obtained with no difficulty. Come with me. I will send for your clothes."

Edith still did not move. Mrs. Cathcart, watching her, saw her features soften one by one, saw the lips part in a smile and the head fall back as peal after peal of clear laughter rang through the room,

"Oh, mother!" The infinite contempt of the voice struck the woman like the lash of a whip. "You don't know me! Go back with you? Divorce him? You're mad! If he had been a rich man indeed I might but for the time being, though I do not love him, and though I should not blame him and do not blame him if he does not love me, my lot is cast with his, my place is here."

"Melodrama!" said the elder woman angrily. "There's a lot of truth and no end of decency in melodrama, Mrs. Cathcart," said Gilbert. His mother-in-law stood livid with rage, then turning, flung out of the room, and they heard the front door slam behind her.

They looked at each other, this strangely-married pair, for the space of a few seconds, and then Gilbert held out his hand.

"Thank you," he said.

The girl dropped her eyes.

"You have nothing to thank me for," she said listlessly. "I have done you too much wrong for one little act to wipe out all the effects of my selfishness."

VI

THE SAFE AGENCY

The City of London is filled, as all the world knows, with flourishing and well-established businesses.

It abounds in concerns which proclaim, either with dignity or flamboyantly, the fact that this shop stood where it did a hundred years ago, and is still being carried on by the legitimate descendants of its founders.

There are companies and syndicates and trading associations housed in ornate and elaborate buildings, suites of offices which come into existence in the spring and fade away to nothingness in the winter, leaving a residue of unpaid petty accounts, and a landlord who has only this satisfaction—that he was paid his rent in advance.

The tragedies of the City of London lay in a large sense round the ugly and unpretentious buildings of the Stock Exchange, and may be found in the seedy sprinkling of people who perambulate the streets round and round that grimy building like so many disembodied spirits.

But the tragic gambler is not peculiar to the metropolis, and the fortunes made and lost in a day or in an hour has its counterpart in every city in the world where stock transactions are conducted. The picturesque sorrows of the City are represented in the popular mind with the human wreckage which strews the Embankment after dark, or goes shuffling along the edges of the pavement with downcast eyes seeking for discarded cigar ends. That is sorrowful enough, though the unhappy objects of our pity are considerably more satisfied with their lot than most people would imagine.

The real tragedy and sorrow is to be found in the hundred and one little businesses which come into existence joyfully, and swallow up the savings of years of some two or three optimistic individuals. The flourishing note-heads which are issued from brand new offices redolent of paint and fresh varnish; the virgin books imposingly displayed upon new shelves; the mass of correspondence which goes daily forth; the booklets and the leaflets; the explanatory tables and all the paraphernalia of the inexperienced advertiser, and the trickle of replies which come back—they are all part of the sad game.

Some firms endeavour to establish themselves with violence, with a flourish of their largest trumpets. Some drift into business noiselessly and in some mysterious way make good. Generally, one may suppose, they came with the invaluable asset of a "connexion," shifting up from the suburbs to a more impressive address.

One of the business which came into existence in London in the year 1910 was a firm which was defined in the telephone book and in the directory as "The St. Bride's Safe Company." It dealt in new and second-hand safes, strong rooms and all the cunning machinery of protection.

In its one show-room were displayed safes of every make, new and old, gratings, burglar alarms, cash boxes, big and small, and the examples of all that iron and steel could do to resist the attention of the professional burglar.

The principal of the business was apparently a Midland gentleman, who engaged a staff; including a manager and a salesman, by advertisement, interviewed the newly-engaged employees in the Midlands, and placed at the disposal of the manager, who came armed with unimpeachable testimonials, a sum of money sufficient to stock the store and carry on the business.

He found more supplies from time to time in addition to the floating stock-in-trade, and though orders came very infrequently, the proprietor of the concern cheerfully continued to pay the large rent and the fairly generous salaries of the staff. The proprietor would occasionally visit the store, generally late at night, because, as he explained, his business in Birmingham required his constant attention.

The new stock would be inspected; there would be a stock-taking of keys—these were usually kept in the private safe of the firm—and the proprietor would invariably express his satisfaction with the progress of the business. The manager himself never quite understood how his chief could make this office pay, but he evidently did a big trade in the provinces, because he was able to keep a large motor lorry and a driver, who from time to time appeared at the Bride Street store, brought a safe which would be unloaded, or carried away some purchased article to its new owners.

The manager, a Mr. Timmings, and a respectable member of Balham society, could only imagine that the provincial branch of the business was fairly extensive. Sometimes the motor lorry would come with every evidence of having travelled for many miles, and it would seem that the business flourished at any rate, at the Birmingham end.

It was the day following the remarkable occurrence which is chronicled in the previous chapter that Gilbert Standerton decided amongst other things to purchase a safe.

He needed one for his home, and there were reasons which need not be particularized why such an article of furniture was necessary. He had never felt the need of a safe before. When he did, he wanted to get one right away. It was unfortunate, or fortunate as the case may be, that this resolve did not come to him until an hour when most dealers in these unusual commodities were closed. It was after six when he arrived in the City.

Mr. Timmings had gone away early that night, but he had left a most excellent deputy. The proprietor had come to London a little earlier that evening, and through the glass street-doors Gilbert saw him and stared. The door was locked when he tried it, and with a cheery smile the new proprietor came forward himself and unbolted it.

"We are closed," he said, "and I am afraid my manager has gone home. Can I do anything for you?"

Gilbert looked at him.

"Yes," he said slowly, "I want to buy a safe."

"Then possibly I can help you," said the gentle-man good-naturedly. "Won't you come in?"

Gilbert entered, and the door was bolted behind him.

"What kind of safe do you want?" asked the man.

"I want a small one," said the other. "I would like a second-hand Chubb if you have one."

"I think I have got the very thing. I suppose you want it for your office?"

Gilbert shook his head.

"No, I want it for my house," he said shortly, "and I would like it delivered almost at once."

He made an inspection of the various receptacles for valuables, and finally made a choice.

He was on his way out, when he saw the great safe which stood at the end of the store.

It was rather out of the ordinary, being about eight feet in height and about that width. It looked for all the world like a great steel wardrobe. Three sets of locks guarded the interior, and there was in addition a small combination lock.

"That is a very handsome safe," said Gilbert.

"Isn't it?" said the other carelessly.

"What is the value of that?"

"It is sold," said the proprietor a little brusquely.

"Sold? I should like to see the interior," said Gilbert.

The man smiled at him and stroked his upturned moustache thoughtfully.

"I am sorry I can't oblige you," he said. "The fact is, the new proprietor took the keys when he completed the purchase."

"That is very unfortunate," said Gilbert, "for this is one of the most interesting safes I have ever seen."

"It is quite usual," said the other briefly. He tapped the sides with his knuckles in a reflective mood. "It is rather an expensive piece of property."

"It looks as if you had it here permanently."

"It does, doesn't it?" said the other absently. "I had to make it comfortable."

He smiled, then he led the way to another part of the store.

Gilbert would have paid by cheque, but something prevented him. He searched his pockets, and found the fifteen pounds which had been asked for the safe.

With a pleasant good night he was ushered out of the shop, and the door was closed behind him.

"Where have I seen your face before?" said the proprietor to himself. Though he was a very clever man in more ways than one, it is a curious fact that he never placed his customer until many months afterwards.

VII

The Bank Smasher

Three men sat in the inner room of a City office. The outer door was locked, the door communicating between the outer office and the sanctum was wide open.

The men sat at a table, discussing a frugal lunch which had been brought in from a restaurant near by, and talking together in low tones.

George Wallis, who spoke with such authority as to suggest that he held a leading position above and before the others, was a man of forty, inclined a little to stoutness, of middle height, and with no distinguishing features save the short bristling moustache and the jet-black eyebrows which gave his face a somewhat sinister appearance. His eyes were tired and lazy, his square jaw bespoke immense determination, and the hands which played idly with a pen were small but strong; they were the hands of an artist, and indeed George Wallis, under one name or another, was known as an artist in his particular profession in every police bureau on the Continent.

Callidino, the little Italian at his side, was neat and dapper. His hair was rather long, he suggested rather the musical enthusiast than the cool-headed man of business. And yet this dapper Italian was known as the most practical of the remarkable trio which for many years had been the terror of every bank president in France. The third was Persh, a stout man with a pleasant florid face, and a trim cavalry moustache, who, despite his bulk, was a man of extraordinary agility, and his escape from Devil's Island and his subsequent voyage to Australia in an open boat will be fresh in the minds of the average newspaper readers.

They made no disguise as to their identities; they did not evade the frank questioning which was their lot when the City Police smelt them out and came in to investigate the affairs of this "outside brokers'" establishment. The members of the City force were a little disappointed to discover that quite a legitimate business was being done. You cannot quarrel even with convicted bank robbers if they choose to get their living by any way which, however much discredited, is within the law; and beyond warning those of their clients with whom they could get in touch that the heads of this remarkable business were notorious criminals, the police must needs sit by and watch, satisfied that sooner or later the men would make a slip that would bring them within the scope of police action.

"And they will have to wait a jolly long time," said Wallis. He looked round his "Board" with an amused smile.

"Have they been in to-day?" asked Callidino.

"They have been in to-day," said Wallis gravely. "They have searched our books and our desks and our clothes, and even the legs of our office stools."

"An indelicate proceeding," said Persh, cheerfully.

"And what did they find, George?" George smiled.

"They found all there was to be found," he said.

"I suppose it was the burglary at the Bond Guarantees that I have been reading about that's excited them," said the Italian coolly.

"I suppose so," said Wallis, with grave indifference. "It is pretty terrible to have names such as we possess. Seriously," he went on, "I am not very much afraid of the police, even suppose there was anything to find. I haven't met one of them who has the intelligence of that cool devil we met at the Foreign Office, when I had to answer some questions about Persh's unique experiences on Devil's Island."

"What was his name?" asked Persh, interested.

"Something associated in my mind with South Africa—oh, yes, Standerton. A cool beast—I met him at Epsom the other day," said Wallis. "He's lost in a place like the Foreign 0ffice. Do you remember that quick run through he gave me, Persh?"

The other nodded.

"Before I knew where I was I admitted that I'd been in Huntingdonshire the same week as Lady Perkinton's jewels were taken. If he'd had another five minutes I guess he'd have known"—he lowered his voice to little more than a whisper—"all this hidden treasure which the English police are seeking was cached."

The men laughed, as at some great joke.

"Talking of cool people," said Wallis, "do you recall that weird devil who held us up in Hatton Garden?"

"Have you found him?" asked Callidino.

George shook his head.

"No," he said slowly, "only I'm rather afraid of him."

Which was a remarkable confession for him to make. He changed the subject abruptly.

"I suppose you people know," said Wallis, "that the police are particularly active just now? I've reason to be aware of the fact, because they have just concluded a most exhaustive search of my private belongings."

He did not exaggerate. The police were, indeed, most eager for some clue to associate these three known criminals with the acts of the past month.

Half an hour later Wallis left the building. He paused in the entrance hall of the big block of offices and lighted a cigar with an air that betokened his peace with the world and his approval of humanity.

As his foot touched the pavement a tall man stepped to his side. Wallis looked up quickly and gave a little nod. "I want you," said the tall man, coldly.

"Do you indeed?" said Wallis with exaggerated interest. "And what may you want with me?"

"You come along with me, and not so much of your lip," said the man.

He called a cab, and the two men were rapidly driven to the nearest City police station. Wallis continued smoking his cigar, without any outward indication of apprehension. He would have chatted very gaily with the officer who had effected his arrest, but the officer himself was in no mood for light humour.

He was hustled into the charge room and brought before the inspector's desk.

That officer looked up with a nod. He was more genial than his captor.

"Well, Wallis," he said with a smile, "we want some information from you."

"You always want information from somebody," said the man with cold insolence. "Have you had another burglary?"

The inspector nodded.

"Tut, tut!" said the prisoner with an affectation of distress, "how very annoying for you Mr. Whitling. I suppose you have got the culprit?" he asked blandly.

"I've got you at present," said the calm inspector. "I should not be surprised if I had also got the culprit. Can you explain where you were last night?"

"With the greatest of pleasure," said Wallis; "I was dining with a friend."

"His name?"

The other shrugged his shoulders. "His name is immaterial. I was dining with a friend whose name does not matter. Put that down, inspector."

"And where were you dining with this unknown friend?" asked the imperturbable official.

Wallis named a restaurant in Wardour Street.

"At what hour were you dining?" asked the inspector patiently.

"Between the hours of eight and eleven," said the man, "as the proprietor of the restaurant will testify."

The inspector smiled to himself. He knew the restaurant and knew the proprietor. His testimony would not carry a great deal of weight with a jury.

"Have you anybody respectable," he asked, "who will vouch for the fact that you were there, other than your unknown friend and Signor Villimicci?"

Wallis nodded. "I might name, with due respect," he said, "Sergeant Colebrook, of the Central Investigation Department of Scotland Yard."

He was annoyingly bland. The inspector looked up sharply.

"Is he going to vouch for you?" he asked.

"He was watching me the whole of the time, disguised, I think, as a gentleman. At least, he was in evening dress, and he was quite different from the waiters. You see, he was sitting down."

"I see," said the inspector. He put down his pen.

"It was rather amusing to be watched by a real detective-sergeant, from that most awe-inspiring wilderness of bricks," the man continued. "I quite liked it, though I am afraid the poor fellow was bored sooner than I was."

"I understand," said the inspector, "that you were being watched from eight o'clock last night till—?" He paused inquiringly.

"Till near midnight, I should imagine. Until our dress-suited detective, looking tragically like a detective all the time, had escorted me to the front door of my flat."

"I can verify that in a minute," said the inspector. "Go into the parade room."

Wallis strolled unconcernedly into the inner room whilst the inspector manipulated the telephone. In five minutes the prisoner was sent for.

"You're all right," said the inspector. "Clean bill for you, Wallis."

"I am glad to hear it," said Wallis. "Very relieved indeed!" He sighed heavily. "Now that I am embarked upon what I might term a legalized form of thefts from the public, it is especially pleasing to me to know that my actions are approved by the police."

"We don't approve of everything you do," said the inspector.

He was an annoying man, Wallis thought; he would neither lose his temper nor be rude.

"You can go now—sorry to have bothered you."

"Don't mention it," said the polite man with a little bow.

"By the way, before you go," said the inspector, "just come into my inner office, will you?"

Wallis followed him. The inspector closed the door behind them. They were alone.

"Wallis, do you know there is a reward of some twelve thousand pounds for the detection of the men engaged in these burglaries?"

"You surprise me," said Mr. Wallis, lifting his eyebrows.

"I don't surprise you," said the inspector; "in fact, you know much more about it than I do. And I tell you this, that we are prepared to go to any lengths to track this gang, or, at any rate, to put an end to its operations. Look here, George," he tapped the other on the chest with his strong, gnarled finger, "is it a scream?"

"A scream?" Mr. Wallis was puzzled innocence itself.

"Will you turn King's evidence?" said the other shortly.

"I should be most happy," said Wallis, with a helpless shrug; "but how can I turn King's evidence about a matter on which I am absolutely uninformed? The reward is monstrously tempting. If I had companions in crime I should need very little persuading. My conscience is a matter of constant adjustment. It is rather like the foot-rule which shoemakers employ to measure their customers' feet—terrifically adjustable. It has a sliding scale which goes up and down."

"I don't want to hear any more about your conscience," said the officer wearily. "Do you scream or don't you?"

"I don't scream," said Mr. Wallis emphatically.

The inspector jerked his head sideways, and with the bow which the invitation had interrupted, Mr. Wallis walked out into the street.

He knew, no one better, how completely every action of his was watched. He knew, even as he left the station, that the seemingly idle loafer on the corner of the street had picked him up, would follow him until he handed him over to yet another plain-clothes officer for observation. From beat to beat, from one end of the City to another, those vigilant eyes would never leave him; whilst he slept, the door, back and front of his lodging would be watched. He could not move without all London—all the London that mattered as far as he was concerned—knowing everything about that move.

His home was the upper part of a house over a tobacconist's in a small street off Charing Cross Road. And to his maisonette he made a leisurely way, not hastening his steps any the more because he knew that on one side of the street an innocent commercial traveller, and on the other a sandwich man apparently trudging homeward with his board, were keeping him under observation. He stopped to buy some cigars in the Charing Cross Road, crossed near the Alhambra, and ten minutes later was unlocking the door of the narrow passage which ran by the side of the shop, and gave him private access to the suite above.

It was a room comfortably furnished and giving evidence of some taste. Large divan chairs formed a feature of the furnishing, and the prints, though few, were interesting by reason of their obvious rarity.

He did not trouble to make an examination of the room, or of the remainder of the maisonette he rented. If the police had been, they had been. If they had not, it did not matter. They could find nothing. He had a good conscience, so far as a man's conscience may be good for fears less for the consequence of his deeds than for the apparent, the obvious, and the discoverable consequences.

He rang a bell, and after a little delay an old woman answered the call.

"Make me some tea, Mrs. Skard," he said. "Has anybody called?"

The old woman looked up to the ceiling for inspiration.

"Only the man about the gas," she said.

"Only the man about the gas," repeated George Wallis admiringly. "Wasn't he awfully surprised to find that we didn't have gas at all?"

The old lady looked at him in some amazement.

"He did say he had come to see about the gas," she said, "and then, when he found we had no gas, he said 'electricity'—a most absent-minded young man."

"They are that way, Mrs. Skard," said her master tolerantly; "they fall in love, don't you know, round about this season of the year, and when their minds become occupied with other and more pleasant thoughts than gas mantles and incandescent lights they become a little confused. I suppose he did not bother you—he told you you need not wait?" he suggested.

"Quite right, sir," said Mrs. Skard. "He said he would do all he had to do without assistance."

"And I will bet you he did it," said George Wallis with boisterous good humour. Undisturbed by the knowledge that his rooms had been searched by an industrious detective, he sat for an hour reading an American magazine. At six o'clock a taxi-cab drove into the street and pulled up before the entrance of his flat. The driver, a stoutish man with a beard, looked helplessly up and down seeking a number, and one of the two detectives who had been keeping observation on the house walked across the road casually towards him.

"Do you want to find a number, mate?" he asked.

"I want No. 43," said the cabman.

"That's it," said the officer.

He saw the cabman ring, and having observed that he entered the door, which was closed behind him, he walked back to his co-worker.

"George is going to take a little taxi drive," he said; "we will see where he goes."

The man who had waited on the other side of the road nodded.

"I don't suppose he will go anywhere worth following, but I have the car waiting round the corner."

"I'll car him," said the second man bitterly. "Did you hear what he told Inspector Whitling of the City Police about me last night?"

The first detective was considerably interested.

"No, I should like to hear."

"Well," began the man, and then thought better of it. It was nothing to his credit that he should keep a man under observation three hours, and that the quarry should be aware all the time that he was being watched.

"Hullo!" he said, as the door of No. 43 opened, "here is our man." He threw a swift glance along the street, and saw that the hired motor-car which had been provided for his use was waiting.

"Here he comes," he said, but it was not the man he expected. The bearded chauffeur came out alone, waved a farewell to somebody in the hallway whom they could not see, and having started his engine with great deliberation, got upon his seat, and the taxi-cab moved slowly away.

"George is not going," said the detective. "That means that we shall have to stay here for another two or three hours—there is his light."

For four long hours they kept their vigil, and never once was a pair of eyes taken from the only door through which George Wallis could make his exit. There was no other way by which he coulld leave, of that they were assured.

Behind the house was a high wall, and unless the man was working in collusion with half the respectable householders, not only in that street but of Charing Cross Road, he could not by any possible chance leave his flat.

At half-past ten the taxi-cab they had seen drove back to the door of the flat, and the driver was admitted. He evidently did not expect to stay long, for he did not switch off his engine; as a matter of fact, he was not absent from his car longer than thirty seconds. He came back almost immediately, climbed up on to his seat and drove away.

"I wonder what the game is?" asked the detective, a little puzzled.

"He has been to take a message somewhere," said the other. "I think we ought to have found out."

Ten minutes later Inspector Goldberg, of Scotland Yard, drove into the street and sprang from his car opposite the men.

"Has Wallis returned?" he asked quickly.

"Returned!" repeated the puzzled detective, "he has not gone out yet."

"Has not gone out!" repeated the inspector with a gasp. "A man answering to his description was seen leaving the City branch of the Goldsmiths' Guild half an hour ago. The safe has been forced and twenty thousand pounds' worth of jewellery has been taken."

There was a little silence.

"Well, sir," said the subordinate doggedly, "one thing I will swear, and it is that George Wallis has not left this house to-night."

"That's true, sir," said the second man. "The sergeant and I have not left this place since Wallis went in."

"But," said the bewildered detective-inspector, "it must be Wallis, no other man could have done the job as he did it."

"It could not have been, sir," persisted the watcher.

"Then who in the name of Heaven did the job?" snapped the inspector.

His underlings wisely offered no solution.

VIII

The Wife Who Did Not Love

Mr. Warrell, of the firm of Warrell & Bird, prided himself upon being a man of the world, and was wont to admit, in a mild spirit of boastfulness—in which even middle-aged and respectable gentlemen occasionally indulge—that he had been in some very awkward situations. He had inferred that he had escaped from those situations with some credit to himself.

Every stockbroker doing a popular and extensive business is confronted sooner or later with the delicate task of explaining to a rash and hazardous speculator exactly how rashly and at what hazard he has invested his money.

Mr. Warrell had had occasion before to break, as gently as it was possible to break, unpleasant news of Mrs. Cathcart's unsuccess. But never before had he been face to face with a situation so full of possibilities for disagreeable consequences as this which now awaited him.

The impassive Cole admitted him, and the face of Cole fell, for he knew the significance of these visits, having learnt in that mysterious way which servants have of discovering the inward secrets of their masters' and mistresses' bosoms,' that the arrival of Mr. Warrell was usually followed by a period of retrenchment, economy and reform.

"Madam will see you at once," was the message he returned with.

A few minutes later Mrs. Cathcart sailed into the drawing-room, a little harder of face than usual, thought Mr. Warrell, and wondered why.

"Well, Warrell," she said briskly, "what machination of the devil has brought you here? Sit down, won't you?"

He seated himself deliberately. He placed his hat upon the floor, and peeling his gloves, deposited them with unnecessary care in the satin-lined interior.

"What is it?" asked Mrs. Cathcart impatiently. "Are those Canadian Pacifics down again?"

"They are slightly up," said Mr. Warrell, with a smile which was intended both to conciliate and to flatter. "I think your view on Canadian Pacifics is a very sound one."

He knew that Mrs. Cathcart would ordinarily desire nothing better than a tribute to her judgment, but now she dismissed the compliment, realizing that he had not come all the way from Throgmorton Street to say kindly things about her perspicacity.

"I will say all that is in my mind," Mr. Warrell went on, choosing his words, and endeavouring by the adoption of a pained smile to express in some tangible form his frankness. "You owe us some seven hundred pounds, Mrs. Cathcart."

She nodded.

"You have ample security," she said.

"That I realize," he agreed, addressing the ceiling; "but the question is whether you are prepared to make good in actual cash the differences which are due to us."

"There is no question at all about it," she said brusquely; "so far as I am concerned, I cannot raise seven hundred shillings."

"Suppose," suggested Mr. Warrell, with his eyes still upraised, "suppose I could find somebody who would be willing to buy your necklace—I think that was the article you deposited with us—for a thousand pounds?"

"It is worth considerably more than that," said Mrs. Cathcart sharply.

"Possibly," said the other, "but I am anxious to keep things out of the paper." He had launched his bombshell.

"Exactly what do you mean?" she demanded, rising to her feet. She stood glowering down at him.

"Do not misunderstand me," he said hastily. "I will explain in a sentence. Your diamond necklace has been stolen from my safe."

"Stolen!" She went white.

"Stolen," said Mr. Warrell, "by a gang of burglars which has been engaged in its operations for the past twelve months in the City of London. You see, my dear Mrs. Cathcart," he went on, "that it is a very embarrassing situation for both of us. I do not want my clients to know that I accept jewels from ladies as collateral security against differences, and you"—he was so rude as to point to emphasize his words—"do not, I imagine, desire your friends to know that it was necessary for you to deposit those jewels." He shrugged his shoulders.

"Of course, I could have reported the matter to the police, sent out a description of the necklace, and possibly recovered the loss from an insurance company, but that I did not wish to do." He might have added, this good business man, that his insurance policy would not have covered such a loss, for when premiums are adjusted to cover the risk of a stockbroker's office, they do not, as a rule, foreshadow the possibility of a jewel robbery.

"I am willing to stand the loss myself," he continued, "that is to say, I am willing to make good a reasonable amount out of my own pocket, as much for your sake as for mine. On the other hand, if you do not agree to my suggestion, I have no other alternative than to report the matter very, very fully, *very* fully," he repeated with emphasis, "to the police and to the press. Now, what do you think?"

Mrs. Cathcart might have said in truth that she did not know what to think. The necklace was a valuable one, and there were other considerations. Mr. Warrell was evidently thinking of its sentimental value, for he went on: "But for the fact that jewels of this kind have associations, I might suggest that your new son-in-law would possibly replace your loss."

She turned upon him with a hard smile.

"My new son-in-law!" she scoffed. "Good Lord!"

Warrell knew Standerton, and regarded him as one of Fortune's favourites, and was in no doubt as to his financial stability. The contempt in the woman's tone shocked him as only a City man can be shocked by a whisper against the credit of gilt-edged stock. For the moment he forgot the object of his visit. He would have liked to have asked for an explanation, but he felt that it did not lie within the province of Mrs. Cathcart's broker to demand information upon her domestic affairs.

"It is a pretty rotten mess you have got me into, Warrell," she said, and got up.

He rose with her, picked up his hat, and exhumed his buried gloves.

"It is very awkward indeed," he said, "tremendously awkward for you, and tremendously awkward for me, my dear Mrs. Cathcart. I am sure you will pity me in my embarrassment."

"I am too busy pitying myself," she said shortly.

She sat in the drawing-room alone after the broker's departure. What should she do? For what Warrell did not know was that the necklace was not hers. It had been one which the old Colonel had had reset for his daughter, and which had been bequeathed to the girl in her father's will.

A family circle which consists of a mother and a daughter exercises communal rights over property which may appear curious to families more extensive in point of number. Though Edith had known the jewel was hers, she had not demurred when her mother had worn it, and had never even hinted that she would prefer to include it amongst the meagre stock of jewellery in her own case.

Yet it had always been known as "Edith's necklace."

Mrs. Cathcart had referred to it herself in these terms, and an uncomfortable feature of their estrangement had been the question of the necklace and its retention by the broker.

Mrs. Cathcart shrugged her shoulders. There was nothing to be done; she must trust to luck. She could not imagine that Edith would ever feel the need of the jewel; yet if her husband was poor, and she was obsessed with this absurd sense of loyalty to the man who had deceived her, there might be a remote possibility that from a sheer quixotic desire to help her husband, she would make inquiries as to the whereabouts of the necklace.

Edith was not like that, thought Mrs. Cathcart. It was a comforting thought as she made her way up the stairs to her room.

She stopped half-way up to allow the maid to overtake her with the letters which had arrived at that moment. With a little start she recognized upon the first of these the handwriting of her daughter, and tore open the envelope. The letter was brief:

DEAR MOTHER (it ran)
"Would you please arrange for me to have the necklace which father left to me. I feel, now, that I must make some sort of display if only for my husband's sake."

The letter dropped from Mrs. Cathcart's hand. She stood on the stairs transfixed.

EDITH STANDERTON WAS SUPERINTENDING THE arrangement of the lunch table when her husband came in. Life had become curiously systematized in the St. John's Wood house.

To neither of the young people had it seemed possible that they could live together as now they did, in perfect harmony, in sympathy, yet with apparently no sign of love or demonstration of affection on either side.

To liken them to brother and sister would be hardly descriptive of their friendship. They lacked the mutual knowledge of things, and the common interest which brother and sister would have. They wanted, too, an appreciation of one another's faults and virtues.

They were strangers, and every day taught each something about the other. Gilbert learnt that this quiet girl, whose sad grey eyes had hinted at tragedy, had a sense of humour, could laugh on little provocation, and was immensely shrewd in her appraisement of humanity.

She, for her part, had found a force she had not reckoned on, a vitality and a doggedness of purpose which she had never seen before their marriage. He could be entertaining, too, in the rare intervals when they were alone together. He was a traveller: had visited Persia, Arabia, and the less known countries of Eastern Asia.

She never referred again to the events of that terrible marriage night. Here, perhaps, her judgment was at fault. She had seen a player with a face of extraordinary beauty, and had given perhaps too much attention to this minor circumstance. Somewhere in her husband's heart was a secret, what that secret was she could only guess. She guessed that it was associated in some way with a woman—therein the woman in her spoke.

She had no feeling of resentment either towards her husband or to the unknown who had sent a message through the trembling strings of her violin upon that wedding night. Only, she told herself, it was "curious." She wanted to know what it was all about. She had the healthy curiosity of the young. The revelation might shock her, might fill her with undying contempt for the man whose name she bore, but she wanted to know.

It piqued her too, after a while, that he should have any secrets from her—a strange condition of mind, remembering the remarkable relationship in which they stood, and yet one quite understandable. Though they had not achieved the friendly and peculiar relationship of man and wife, there had grown up between them a friendship which the girl told herself (and did her best to believe) was of a more enduring character than that which marriage *qua* marriage could produce. It was a comradeship in which much was taken for granted; she took for granted that he loved her, and entered into the marriage with no other object. That was a comforting basis for friendship with any woman.

For his part, he took it for granted that she had a soul above deception; that she was frank even though in her frankness she wounded him almost to death. He detected in that an unusual respect for himself, though in his more logical mood he argued she would have acted as honourably to any man.

She herself wove into the friendship a peculiar sexless variety of romance—sexless, since she thought she saw in it an accomplished ideal towards which the youth of all ages have aspired without any conspicuous success. There is no man or woman in the world who does not think that the chance in a million may be his or hers; there is no human creature so diffident that it does not imagine in its favour is created exception to evident and universal rules.

Plato may have stopped dead in his conduct of other friendships, his philosophies may have frizzled hopelessly and helplessly, and have been evaporated to thin vapour before the fire of natural love. A thousand witnesses may rise to testify to the futility of friendship in two people of opposite sex, but there always is the "you" and the "me" in the world, who defies experience, and comes with sublime faith to show how different will be the result to that which has attended all previous experiments.

As she told herself, if there had been the slightest spark of love in her bosom for this young man who had come into her life with some suddenness, and had gone out in a sense so violently, only to return in another guise; if there had been the veriest smouldering ember of the thing called love in her heart; she would have been jealous, just a little jealous, of the interests which drew him away from her every night, and often brought him home when the grey dawn was staining the blue of the East.

She had watched him once from her window, and had wondered vaguely what he found to do at night.

Was he seeking relaxation from an intolerable position? He never gave her the impression that it was intolerable. There was comfort in that thought. Was there—somebody else? Here was a question to make her knit her brows, this loveless wife.

Once she found herself, to her intense amazement, on the verge of tears at the thought. She went through all the stages of doubt and decision, of anger and contrition, which a young wife more happily circumstanced might have experienced.

Who was the violin player with the beautiful face? What part had she taken in Gilbert's life?

One thing she did know, her husband was gambling on the Stock Exchange. At first she did not realize that he could be so commonplace. She had always regarded him as a man to whom vulgar money-grabbing would be repugnant. He had surrendered his position at the Foreign

Office; he was now engaged in some business which neither discussed. She thought many things, but until she discovered the contract note of a broker upon his desk, she had never suspected success on the Stock Exchange as, the goal of his ambition.

This transaction seemed an enormous one to her.

There were tens of thousands of shares detailed upon the note. She knew very little about the Stock Exchange, except that there had been mornings when her mother had been unbearable as a result of her losses. Then it occurred to her, if he were in business—a vague term which meant anything—she might do something more than sit at home and direct his servants.

She might help him also in another way. Business men have expedient dinners, give tactful theatre parties. And many men have succeeded because they have wives who are wise in their generation.

It was a good thought. She held a grand review of her wardrobe, and posted the letter which so completely destroyed her mother's peace of mind.

Gilbert had been out all the morning, and he came back from the City looking rather tired.

An exchange of smiles, a little strained and a little hard on one side, a little wistful and a little sad on the other, had become the conventional greeting between the two, so too had the inquiry, "Did you sleep well?" which was the legitimate property of whosoever thought of this original question.

They were in the midst of lunch when she asked suddenly: "Would you like me to give a dinner party?"

He looked up with a start.

"A dinner party!" he said incredulously; then, seeing her face drop, and realizing something of the sacrifice which she might be making he added: "I think it is an excellent idea. Whom would you like to invite?"

"Any friends you have," she said, "that rather nice man Mr. Frankfort, and—who else?" she asked.

He smiled a little grimly.

"I think that rather nice man Mr. Frankfort about exhausts the sum of my friends," he said with a little laugh. "We might ask Warrell."

"Who is Warrell? Oh, I know," she said quickly, "he is mother's broker."

He looked at her curiously.

"Your mother's broker," he repeated slowly, "is he really?"

"Why?" she asked.

"Why what?" he evaded.

"Why did you say that so queerly?"

"I did not know that I did," he said carelessly, "only somehow one doesn't associate your mother with a broker. Yet I suppose she finds an agent necessary in these days. You see, he is my broker, too."

"Who else?" she asked.

"On my side of the family," he said with mock solemnity, "I can think of nobody. What about your mother?"

"I could ask one or two nice people," she went on, ignoring the suggestion.

"What about your mother?" he said again.

She looked up, her eyes filled with tears.

"Please do not be horrid," she said. "You know that is impossible."

"Not at all, "he answered cheerfully. "I made the suggestion in all good faith; I think it is a good one. After all, there is no reason why this absurd quarrel should go on. I admit I felt very sore with her; but then I even felt sore with you!" He looked at her not unkindly. "The soreness is gradually wearing away," he said. He spoke half to himself, though he looked at the girl. It seemed to her that he was trying to convince himself of something in which he did not wholly believe.

"It is extraordinary," he said, "how little things, little worries, and petty causes for unhappiness disappear in the face of a really great trouble."

"What is your great trouble?" she asked, quick to seize the advantage which he had given her in that unguarded moment.

"None," he said.

His tone was a little louder than usual, it was almost defiant.

"I am speaking hypothetically. I have no trouble save the very obvious troubles of life," he went on. "You were a trouble to me for quite a little time, but you are not any more."

"I am glad you said that," she said softly. "I want to be real good friends with you, Gilbert—I want to be a real good friend to you, I have made rather a hash of your life, I'm afraid."

She had risen from the table and stood looking down at him. He shook his head.

"I do not think you have," he said, "not the hash that you imagine. Other circumstances have conspired to disfigure what was a pleasant outlook. It is unfortunate that our marriage has not proved to be all that

I dreamt it would be, but then dreams are very unstable foundations to the fabric of life. You would not think that I was a dreamer, would, you?" he said quickly with that ready smile of his, those eyes that creased into little lines at the corners. "You would not imagine me as a romancist, though I am afraid I was."

"You are, you mean," she corrected.

He made no reply to that.

The question of the dinner came up later, when he was preparing to go out.

"You would not like to stay and talk it over, I suppose," she suggested a little timidly. He hesitated. "There is nothing I should like better," he said, "but"—he looked at his watch. She pressed her lips together, and for one moment felt a wave of unreasoning anger sweeping over her.

It was absurd, of course; he always went out at this time, and there was really no reason why he should stay in.

"We can discuss it another time," she said coldly, and left him without a further word.

He waited until he heard the door close in her room above, and then he went out with a little smile in which there were tears almost, but in which there was no merriment.

He left the house at a propitious moment; had he waited another five minutes he would have met his mother-in-law. Mrs. Cathcart had made up her mind to "own up," and had come in person to make the confession.

It was a merciful providence, so she told herself, that had taken Gilbert out of the way; that he had gone out she discovered before she had been in the house four minutes, and she discovered it by the very simple process of demanding from Gilbert's servant whether his master was at home.

Edith heard of her mother's arrival without surprise. She supposed that Mrs. Cathcart had come to hand the necklace to its lawful owner. She felt some pricking of conscience as she came down the stairs to meet her mother; had she not been unnecessarily brusque in her demand! She was a tender soul, and had a proper and natural affection for the elder woman. The fear that she might have hurt her feelings, and that that hurt might be expressed at the interview, gave her a little qualm as she opened the drawing-room door.

Mrs. Cathcart was coolness itself. You might have thought that never a scene had occurred between these two women which could be remembered with unkindliness. No reference was made to the past, and Edith was glad. It was not her desire that she should live on bad terms with her mother. She understood her too well, which was unfortunate for both; and it would be all the happier for them if they could maintain some pretence of friendship.

Mrs. Cathcart came straight to the point.

"I suppose you know why I have called," she said, after the first exchange.

"I suppose you have brought the necklace," said the girl with a smile. "You do not think I am horrid to ask for it, but I feel I ought to do something for Gilbert."

"I think you might have chosen another subject for your first letter," said the elder woman grimly, "but still—"

Edith made no reply. It was useless to argue with her mother. Mrs. Cathcart had a quality which is by no means rare in the total of human possessions, the quality of putting other people in the wrong.

"I am more sorry," Mrs. Cathcart resumed, "because I am not in a position to give you your necklace."

The girl stared at her mother in wonder.

"Why! Whatever do you mean, mother?" she asked.

Mrs. Cathcart carefully avoided her eyes.

"I have had losses on the Stock Exchange," she said. "I suppose you know that your father left us just sufficient to starve on, and whatever luxury and whatever comfort you have had has been due to my own individual efforts? I have lost a lot of money over Canadian Pacifics," she said bluntly.

"Well?" asked the girl, wondering what was coming next, and fearing the worst.

"I made a loss of seven hundred pounds with a firm of stockbrokers," Mrs. Cathcart continued, "and I deposited your necklace with the firm as security.

The girl gasped.

"I intended, of course, redeeming it, but an unfortunate thing happened—the safe was burgled and the necklace was stolen."

Edith Standerton stared at the other. The question of the necklace did not greatly worry her, yet she realized now that she had depended rather more upon it than she had thought. It was a little nest-egg against a bad time, which, if Gilbert spoke the truth, might come at any moment.

"It cannot be helped," she said.

She did not criticize her mother, or offer any opinion upon the impropriety of offering as security for debt articles which are the property of somebody else. Such criticism would have been wasted and the effort would have been entirely superfluous.

"Well," asked Mrs. Cathcart, "what have you got to say?"

The girl shrugged her shoulders.

"What can I say, mother? The thing is lost, and there is an end to it. Do the firm offer any compensation?"

She asked the question innocently: it occurred to her as a wandering thought that possibly something might be saved from the wreck.

Mrs. Cathcart shot a swift glance at her. Had that infernal Warrell been communicating with her? She knew that Warrell was a friend of Edith's husband. It would be iniquitous of him if he had.

"Some compensation was offered," she answered carelessly, "quite inadequate; the matter is not settled yet, but I will let you know how it develops."

"What compensation do they offer?" asked Edith, Mrs. Cathcart hesitated.

"A thousand pounds," she said reluctantly.

"A thousand pounds!"

The girl was startled, she had no idea the necklace was of that value.

"That means of course," Mrs. Cathcart hastened to explain, "seven hundred pounds out of my pocket and three hundred pounds from the broker."

The girl smiled inwardly.

"Seven hundred pounds from my pocket" meant, "if you ask for the full value you will rob me."

"And there is three hundred pounds due. I think I had better have that."

"Wait a little," said Mrs. Cathcart, "they may recover the necklace, anyway; they want me to give a description of it. What do you think?"

The girl shook her head.

"I do not think I should like that," she said quietly. "Questions might be asked, and I should not like people to know either that the necklace was mine, or that my mother had deposited it as security against her debts."

Here was the new Edith with a vengeance.

Mrs. Cathcart stared at her.

"Edith," she said severely, "that sounds a little impertinent."

"I dare say it does, mother," said the girl; "but what am I to do? What am I to say? There are the facts fairly apparent to you and to me: the necklace is stolen, and it may possibly never be recovered, and I am not going to expose either my loss or your weakness on the remote possibility of getting back an article of jewellery which probably by this time is in the melting-pot and the stones dispersed."

"You know a great deal about jewels and jewel-robbers," said her mother with a little sneer. "Has Gilbert been enlarging your education?"

"Curiously enough, he has," said her daughter calmly; "we discuss many queer things."

"You must have very pleasant evenings," said the elder woman dryly.

She rose to go, looking at her watch. "I am sorry I cannot stay," she said, "but I am dining with some people. I suppose you would not like to come along? It is quite an informal affair; as a matter of fact, the invitation included you."

"And Gilbert?" asked the girl. The woman smiled.

"No, it did not exactly include Gilbert," she said. "I have made it pretty clear that invitations to me are acceptable only so long as the party does not include your husband."

The girl drew herself up stiffly, and the elder woman saw a storm gathering in her eyes.

"I do not quite understand you. Do you mean that you have gone round London talking unkindly about my husband?"

"Of course I have," said Mrs. Cathcart virtuously. "I do not know about having gone round London, but I have told those people who are intimate friends of mine and who are naturally interested in my affairs."

"You have no right to speak," said the girl angrily; "it is disgraceful of you. You have made your mistake and you must abide by the consequence. I also have made a mistake and I cheerfully accept my lot. If it hurts you that I am married to a man who despises me, how much more do you think it hurts me?"

Mrs. Cathcart laughed.

"I assure you," she smiled, "that though many thoughts disturb my nights, the thought that your husband has no particular love for you is not one of them; what does wake me up with a horrid feeling is the knowledge that so far from being the rich man I thought he was, he is practically penniless. What madness induced him to give up his work at the Foreign Office?"

"You had better ask him," said the girl with malice, "he will be in in a few moments."

It needed only this to hasten Mrs. Cathcart's departure, and Edith was left alone.

Edith Dined alone that night.

At first she had welcomed with a sense of infinite relief these solitary dinners. She was a woman of considerable intelligence, and she had faced the future without illusion.

She realized that there might come a time when she and Gilbert would live together in perfect harmony, though without the essential sympathies which husband and wife should mutually possess. She was willing to undergo the years of probation; and it made it all the easier for her if business or pleasure kept them apart during the embarrassing hours between dinner and bed-time.

But to-night, for the first time, she was lonely.

She felt the need of him, the desire for his society, the cheer and the vitality of him.

There were moments when he was bright and happy and flippant, as she had known him at his best. There were other moments too, terrible and depressing moments, when she never saw him, when he shut himself in his study and she only caught a glimpse of his face by accident. She went through her dinner alternately reading and thinking.

A book lay upon the table by her side, but she did not turn one page. The maid was clearing the entree when Edith Standerton looked up with a start.

"What is it?" she said.

"What, madam?" asked the girl.

Outside the window Edith could hear the sound of music, a gentle, soft cadence of sound, a tiny wail of melodious tragedy. She rose from the table, walked across to the window and pulled aside the blinds. Outside a girl was playing a violin. In the light which a street lamp afforded Edith recognized the player of the "Melody in F."

IX

Edith Meets the Player

E dith turned to her waiting maid. "Go out and bring the girl in at once," she said quietly.

"Which girl, madam?" asked the startled servant.

"The girl who is playing," said Edith. "Hurry please, before she goes."

She was filled with sudden determination to unravel this mystery. She might be acting disloyally to her husband, but she adjusted any fear she may have had on the score with the thought that she might also be helping him. The maid returned in a few minutes and ushered in a girl.

Yes, it was the girl she had seen on her wedding night. She stood now, framed in the doorway, watching her hostess with frank curiosity.

"Won't you come in?" said Edith. "Have you had any dinner?"

"Thank you very much," said the girl, "we do not take dinner, but I had a very good tea."

"Will you sit down for a little while?"

With a graceful inclination of her head the girl accepted the invitation. Her voice was free from the foreign accent which Edith had expected. She was indubitably English, and there was a refinement in her tone which Edith had not expected to meet.

"I suppose you wonder why I have sent for you?" asked Edith Standerton.

The girl showed two rows of white, even teeth in a smile.

"When people send for me," she said demurely, "it is either to pay me for my music, or to bribe me to desist!"

There was frank merriment in her eyes, her smile lit up the face and changed its whole aspect.

"I am doing both," said Edith, "and I also want to ask you something. Do you know my husband?"

"Mr. Standerton," said the girl, and nodded; "yes, I have seen him, and I have played to him."

"Do you remember a night in June," asked Edith, her heart beating faster at the memory, "when you came under this window and played"— she hesitated—"a certain tune?"

The girl nodded.

"Why, yes," she said in surprise, "of course I remember that night of all nights."

"Why of all nights?" asked Edith quickly.

"Well, you see, as a rule my grandfather plays for Mr. Standerton, and that night he was ill. He caught a bad chill on Derby Day—we were wet through by the storm, for we were playing at Epsom—and I had to come here and deputize for him. I did not want to go out a bit that night," she confessed with a bitter laugh, "and I hate the tune; but it was all so mysterious and so romantic."

"Just tell me what was 'mysterious' and what was 'romantic,'" said Edith.

The coffee came in at that moment, and she poured a cup for her visitor.

What is your name?" she asked.

"May Wing," said the girl.

"Now tell me, May, all you know," said Edith, as she passed the coffee, "and please believe it is not out of curiosity that I ask you."

"I will tell you everything," said the girl nodding.

"I remember that day particularly because I had been to the Academy of Music to take my lesson—you would not think we could afford that, but granny absolutely insists upon it. I got back home rather tired. Grandfather was lying down on the couch. We live at Hoxton. He seemed a little troubled. 'May,' he said, 'I want you to do something for me to-night,' Of course, I was quite willing and happy to do it."

The girl stopped suddenly.

"Why, how extraordinary," she said, "I believe I have got proof in my pocket of all that I say."

She had hanging from her waist a little bag of the same material as her dress, and this she opened and searched inside.

She brought out an envelope.

"I will not show you this yet," she said, "but I will tell you what happened. Grandfather, as I was saying, was very troubled, and he asked me if I would do something for him, knowing of course that I would. "'I have had a letter which I cannot make head or tail of,' he said, and he showed me this letter."

The girl held out the envelope.

Edith took it and removed the card inside.

"Why, this is my husband's writing!" she cried.

"Yes," nodded the girl."

It bore the Doncaster postmark, and the letter was brief. It was addressed to the old musician, and ran:

> Enclosed you will find a postal order for one pound. On receipt of this go to the house of Mr. Standerton between the hours of half-past seven and eight o'clock and play Rubenstein's 'Melody in F.' Ascertain if he is at home, and, if he is not, return the next night and play the same tune at the same hour.

That was all.

"I cannot understand it," said Edith puzzled. "What does it mean?"

The girl musician smiled.

"I should like to know what it meant too. You see, I am as curious as you, and think it is a failing which all women share."

"And you do not know why this was sent?"

"No."

"Or what is its meaning?"

Again the girl shook her head.

Edith looked at the envelope and examined the postmark.

It was dated May the twenty-fourth.

"May the twenty-fourth," she repeated to herself.

"Just wait one moment," she said, and ran upstairs to her bedroom.

Feverishly she unlocked her bureau and took out the red-covered diary in which she had inscribed the little events of her life in Portland Square. She turned to May the twenty-fourth. There were only two entries. The first had to do with the arrival of a new dress, but the second was very emphatic:

> G.S. came at seven o'clock and stayed to dinner. Was very absent-minded and worried, apparently. He left at ten. Had a depressing evening.

She looked at the envelope again.

"Doncaster, 7.30," it said.

So the letter had been posted a hundred and eighty miles away half an hour after he had arrived in Portland Square. She went back to the dining-room bewildered, but she controlled her agitation in the presence of the girl.

"I must really patronize one of the arts," she smiled.

She took a half-sovereign from her purse and handed it to May.

"Oh, really," protested the little musician.

"No, take it, please. You have given me a great deal to think about. Has Mr. Standerton ever referred to this incident since?"

"Never," said the girl. "I have never seen him since, except once when I was on the top of an omnibus."

A few minutes later the girl left.

Here was food for imagination, suffcient to occupy her mind, thought Edith.

"What did it mean?" she asked. "What mystery was behind all this?"

Now that she recalled the circumstances, she remembered that Gilbert had been terribly distrait that night; he was nervous, she had noticed his hand shaking, and had remarked to her mother upon his extraordinary absent-mindedness.

And if he had expected the musician to call, and if he himself had specified what tune should be played, why had its playing produced so terrible an effect upon him? He was no *poseur*. There was nothing theatrical in his temperament. He was a musician, and loved music as he loved nothing else in the world save her!

She thought of that reservation with some tenderness. He had loved her then, whatever might be his feelings now, and the love of a strong man does not easily evaporate, nor is it destroyed at a word. Since their marriage his piano had not been opened. He had been a subscriber to almost every musical event in London, yet he had not attended a single concert, not once visited the opera.

With the playing of the "Melody in F," it seemed to her that there had ended one precious period of his life. She had suggested once that they should go to a concert which all musical London was attending.

"Perhaps you would like to go," he had suggested, briefly. "I am afraid I shall be rather busy that night." This, after he had told her not once, but a score of times that music expressed to him every message and every emotion in language clearer than the printed word.

What did it mean? She was seized with a sudden energy, a sudden desire for knowledge—she wanted to share a greater portion of his life. What connexion had this melody with the sudden change that had come to him? What association had it with the adoption of this strenuous life of his, lately? What had it to do with his resignation from the Foreign Office and from his clubs?

She was certain there must be some connection, and she was determined to discover what. As she was in the dark she could not help him. She knew instinctively that to ask him would be of little use. He was of the type who preferred to play a lone hand.

She was his wife, she owed him something. She had brought unhappiness into his life, and she could do no less than strive to help him. She would want money. She sat down and wrote a little note to her mother. She would take the three hundred pounds which were due from the broker; she even went so far as to hint that, if this matter were not promptly settled by her parent, she herself would see Mr. Warrell and conclude negotiations.

She had read in the morning paper the advertisement of a private detective agency, and for a while she was inclined to engage a man. But what special qualifications did private detectives have that she herself did not possess? It required no special training to use one's brains and to exercise one's logical faculties.

She had found a mission in life—the solution of this mystery which surrounded her husband like a cloud. She found herself feeling cheerful at the prospect of the work to which she had set her hand. "You should find yourself an occupation," Gilbert had said in his hesitating fashion. She smiled, and wondered exactly what he would think if he knew the occupation she had found.

THE LITTLE HOUSE IN HOXTON which sheltered May and her grandfather was in a respectable little street, in the main inhabited by members of the artisan class. Small and humble as the dwelling was it was furnished in perfect taste. The furniture was old in the more valuable and more attractive sense of the word.

Old man Wing propped up in his arm-chair sat by a small fire in the room which served as kitchen and dining-room. May was busy with her sewing.

"My dear," said the old man in his gentle voice, "I do not think you had better go out again to-night."

"Why not, grandpa?" asked the girl without looking up from her work.

"Well, it is probably selfishness on my part," he said, "but somehow I do not want to be left alone. I am expecting a visitor."

"A visitor!"

Visitors were unusual at No. 9 Pexton Street, Hoxton. The only visitor they knew was the rent man who called with monotonous regularity every Monday morning.

"Yes," said her grandfather hesitatingly, "I think you remember the gentleman; you saw him some time ago."

"Not Mr. Standerton?" The old man shook his head.

"No, not Mr. Standerton," he said, "but you will recall how at Epsom a rather nice man helped you out of a crowd after a race?"

"I remember," she said.

"His name is Wallis," said the old man, "and I met him by accident today when I was shopping."

"Wallis," she repeated.

Old Wing was silent for a while, then he asked:

"Do you think, my dear, we could take a lodger?"

"Oh, no," protested the girl. "Please not!"

"I find the rent rather heavy," said her grandfather, shaking his head, "and this Mr. Wallis is a quiet sort of person and not likely to give us any trouble."

Still the girl was not satisfied.

"I would rather we didn't," she said. "I am quite sure we can earn enough to keep the house going without that kind of assistance. Lodgers are nuisances. I do not suppose Mrs. Gamage would like it."

Mrs. Gamage was the faded neighbour who came in every morning to help straighten the house.

The girl saw the old man's face fall and went round to him, putting her arm around his shoulder.

"Do not bother, grandpa dear," she said, "if you want a lodger you shall have one. I think it would be rather nice to have somebody in the house who could talk to you when I am out."

There was a knock at the door.

"That must be our visitor," she said, and went to open it.

She recognized the man who stood in the doorway. "May I come in?" he asked. "I wanted to see your grandfather on a matter of business. I suppose you are Miss Wing."

She nodded.

"Come in," she said, and led the way to the kitchen.

"I will not keep you very long," said Mr. Wallis. "No, thank you, I will stand while I am here. I want to find a quiet lodging for a friend of mine. At least," he went on, "he is a man in whom I am rather interested, a very quiet sobersides individual who will be out most of the day, and possibly out most of the night too." He smiled. "He is a—" He hesitated. "He is a taxi-cab driver, to be exact," he said, "though he does not want this fact to be well known because he has seen—er— better days."

"We have only a very small room we can give your friend," said May, "perhaps you would like to see it."

She took him up to the spare bedroom, which they had used on very rare occasions for the accommodation of the few visitors who had been their guests. The room was neat and clean, and George Wallis nodded approvingly.

"I should like nothing better than this for myself," he said. He himself suggested a higher price than she asked, and insisted upon paying a month in advance.

"I have told the man to call, he ought to be here by now; if you do not mind, I will wait for him."

It was not a long wait, for in a few minutes there arrived the new lodger. He was a burly man with a heavy black beard, clipped short, and the fact that he was somewhat taciturn and short of speech rather enhanced his value as a lodger than otherwise.

Wallis took farewell of the old man and his granddaughter, and accompanied by the man, whose name was given somewhat unpromisingly as Smith, he walked to the end of the street.

He had something to say, and that something was important.

"I have got you this place, Smithy," he said, as they walked slowly towards Hoxton High Street, "because it is quiet and fairly safe. The people are respected, and nobody will bother you."

"They are not likely to worry me in any way, are they?" said the man addressed as Smith.

"Not at present," replied the other, "but I do not know exactly how things are going to develop. I am worried."

"What are you worried about?"

George Wallis laughed a little helplessly.

"Why do you ask such stupid questions?" he said with good-natured irritation. "Don't you realize what has happened? Somebody knows our game."

"Well, why not drop it?" asked the other quietly.

"How can we drop it? My dear good chap, though in twelve months we have accumulated a store of movable property sufficiently valuable to enable us all to retire upon, there is not one of us who is willing at this moment to cut out—it would take us twelve months to get rid of the loot," he said thoughtfully.

"I do not exactly know where it is," said Smith with a little smile.

"Nobody knows that but me," replied Wallis with a little frown, "that is the worrying part of it. I feel the whole responsibility upon me. Smithy, we are being really watched."

The other smiled.

"That isn't unusual," he said. But Wallis was very serious.

"Whom do you suspect?" he asked.

The other did not answer for a moment.

"I do not suspect, I know," he said. "A few months ago, when Calli and I were doing a job in Hatton Garden we were interrupted by the arrival of a mysterious gentleman, who watched me open the safe and disappeared immediately afterwards. At that time he did not seem to be particularly hostile or have any ulterior motive in view. Now, for some reason which is best known to himself, he is working against us. That is the man we have got to find."

"But how?"

"Put an advertisement in the paper," said the other sarcastically: "Will the gentleman who dogs Mr. Wallis kindly reveal his identity, and no further action will be taken."

"But seriously!" said the other. "We have got to discover who he is, there must be some way of trapping him; but the only thing to do, and I must do it for my own protection, is to get you all together and share out. We had better meet."

Smith nodded. "When?"

"To-night," said Wallis. "Meet me at the. . ."

He mentioned the name of a restaurant near Regent Street.

It was, curiously enough, the very restaurant where Gilbert Standerton invariably dined alone.

X

The Necklace

Mrs. Cathcart was considerably surprised to receive an invitation to the dinner. She had that morning sent her daughter a cheque for three hundred pounds which she had received from her broker, but as their letters had crossed one event had no connexion with the other.

She did not immediately decide to accept the invitation; she was not sure as to the terms on which she desired to remain with her new son-in-law.

She was, however (whatever might be her faults), a good strategist, and there was nothing to be gained by declining the invitation, and there might be some advantage in accepting.

She was surprised to meet Mr. Warrell, surprised and a little embarrassed; but now that her daughter knew everything there was no reason in the world why she should feel uncomfortable.

She took him in charge, as was her wont, from the moment she met him in the little drawing-room at the St. John's Wood house.

It was a pleasant dinner. Gilbert made a perfect host, he seemed to have revived within himself something of the old gay spirit. Warrell, remembering all that Mrs. Cathcart had told him, was on the *qui vive* to discover some evidence of dissension between husband and wife; the more anxious, perhaps, since he was before everything a professional man, to find justification for Mrs. Cathcart's suggestion, that all was not going well with Gilbert.

Leslie Frankfort, a member of the party, had been questioned by his partner without the elder man eliciting any information which might help to dispel the doubt that was in Warrell's mind.

Leslie Frankfort, that cheerful youth, was as much in the dark as his partner. It gave him some satisfaction to discover that at any rate there was no immediate prospect of ruin in his friend's *menage.*

The dinner was perfect, the food rare and chosen by an epicure, which indeed it was, as Gilbert had assisted his wife to prepare the menu.

The talk drifted idly, as talk does, at such a dinner party, around the topics which men and women were discussing at a thousand other dinner tables in England, and in the natural course of events it turned upon the startling series of burglaries that had been committed recently in London. That the talk should take this drift was more natural, perhaps, because Mrs. Cathcart had very boldly introduced the subject with reference to the burglary at Warrell's.

"No, indeed," said Mr. Warrell, shaking his head, "I regret to say we have no clue. The police have the matter in hand, but I'm afraid we shall never find the man, or men, who perpetrated the crime."

"I don't suppose they would be of much service to you if you found them," said Gilbert quietly.

"I don't know," demurred the other. "We might possibly get the jewels back."

Gilbert Standerton laughed, but stopped in the middle of it.

"Jewels?" he said.

"Don't you remember, Gilbert?" Leslie broke in, "I told you that we had a necklace in the safe, the property of a client, one of those gambling ladies' who patronize us."

A warning glance from his partner arrested him. The gambling lady herself was rather red, and shot a malevolent glance at the indiscreet young man.

"The necklace was mine," she said acidly.

"Oh!" said Leslie, and found the conversation of no great interest to him.

Gilbert did not smile at his friend's embarrassment.

"A necklace," he repeated, "how curious—yours?"

"Mine," repeated Mrs. Cathcart. "I placed it with Warrell's for security. Precious fine security it proved," she added. Warrell was all apologies. He was embarrassed for more reasons than one. He was very annoyed indeed with the indiscreet youth who owed his preponderant interest in the firm the more by reason of his dead father's shares in the business than to any extent to his intelligence or his usefulness.

"Exactly what kind of necklace was it?" continued Gilbert. "I did not see a description."

"No description was given," said Mr. Warrell, coming to the relief of his client, whom he knew from infallible signs was fast losing her temper. "We wished to keep the matter quiet, so that if should not get into the papers."

Edith tactfully turned the conversation, and in a few minutes they were deep in the discussion of a question which has never failed to excite great interest—the abstract problem of the church. Mrs. Cathcart, it may be remarked in passing, was a churchwoman of some standing, a leader amongst a certain set, and an extreme ritualist. Add to this element the broad Nonconformity of Mr. Warrell, the frank scepticism of Leslie, and there were all the ingredients for an argument, which in less refined circles might develop to a sanguinary conclusion.

Edith at least was relieved, however drastic the remedy might be, and was quite prepared to disestablish the Church of Wales, or if necessary the Church of England, rather than see the folly of her mother exposed.

Despite argument, dogmatism of Mrs. Cathcart, philippic of Leslie, and the good-natured tolerance of Mr. Warrell, this latter a most trying attitude to combat, the dinner ended pleasantly, and they adjourned to the little drawing-room upstairs.

"I'm afraid I shall have to leave you," said Gilbert. It was nearly ten o'clock, and he had already warned his wife of an engagement he had made for a later hour.

"I believe old Gilbert is a journalist in these days," said Leslie. "I saw you the other night in Fleet Street, didn't I?"

"No," replied Gilbert, shortly.

"Then it must have been your double," said the other.

Edith had not followed the party upstairs. Just before dinner Gilbert had asked her, with some hesitation, to make him up a packet of sandwiches.

"I may be out the greater part of the night," he said. "A man wants me to motor down to Brighton to meet somebody."

"Will you be out all night?" she had asked, a little alarmed.

He shook his head.

"No, I shall be back by four," he said.

She might have thought it was an unusual hour to meet people, but she made no comment.

As her little party had gone upstairs she had remembered the sandwiches, and went down into the kitchen to see if cook had cut and laid them ready. She wrapped them up for him and packed them into a little flat sandwich case she had, and then made her way back to the hall.

His coat was hanging on a rack, and she had to slip them into the pocket. There was a newspaper in the way; she pulled it out, and there was something else, something loose and uneven. She smiled at his untidiness, and put in her hand to remove the debris.

Her face changed.

What was it?

Her fingers closed round the object in the bottom of the pocket, and she drew it out. There in the palm of her hand, clearly revealed by the electric lamp above her head, shone her diamond necklace!

For a moment the little hall swayed, but she steadied herself with an effort.

Her necklace!

There was no doubt—she turned it over with trembling fingers.

How had he got it? Where did it come from?

A thought had struck her, but it was too horrible for her to give it expression.

Gilbert a burglar! It was absurd. She tried to smile, but failed. Almost every night he had been out, every night in the week in which this burglary had been committed.

She heard a footstep on the stairs, and thrust the necklace into the bosom of her dress. It was Gilbert. He did not notice her face, then: "Gilbert," she said, and something in her voice warned him.

He turned, peering down at her.

"What is wrong?" he asked.

"Will you come into the dining-room for a moment?" she said.

Her voice sounded far away to her. She felt it was not she who was speaking, but some third person.

He opened the door of the dining-room and walked in. The table was spread with the debris of the dinner which had just been concluded. The rosy glow of the overhead lamp fell upon a pretty chaos of flowers and silver and glass. He closed the door behind him.

"What is it?" he asked.

"This," she replied quietly, and drew the necklace from her dress.

He looked at it. Not a muscle of his face moved.

"That?" he said. "Well, what is that?"

"My necklace!"

"Your necklace," he repeated dully. "Is that the necklace that your mother lost?"

She nodded, not trusting herself to speak.

"How very curious." He reached out his hand and took it from her and examined the diamond pendant.

"And that is your necklace," he said. "Well, that is a remarkable coincidence."

"Where did you get it?" she asked. He did not make any reply. He was looking at her with a stony stare in which there was neither expression nor encouragement for speculation.

"Where did I get it?" he repeated calmly. "Who told you that I'd got it?"

"I found it in your pocket," she said breathlessly. "Oh, Gilbert, there is no use in denying that you had it there or you knew it was there. Where did you get it?"

Another pause, then came the answer.

"I found it." It was lame and unconvincing, and he knew it.

She repeated the question.

"I am not prepared to tell you," he said calmly. "You think I stole it, I suppose? You probably imagine that I am a burglar?"

He smiled, but the lips that curved in laughter were hard.

"I can see that in your eyes," he went on. "You explain my absence from home, my retirement from the Foreign Office, by the fact that I have taken up a more lucrative profession." He laughed aloud. "Well, I have," he said. "It is not exactly burglary. I assure you," he went on with mock solemnity, "that I have never burgled a safe in my life. I give you my word of honour that I have never stolen a single article of any—"

He stopped himself—he might say too much.

But Edith grasped at the straw he offered her.

"Oh, you do mean that, don't you?" she said eagerly, and laid her two hands on his breast. "You really mean it? I know it is stupid of me, foolish and horribly disloyal—common of me, anything you like, to suspect you of so awful a thing, but it did seem—it did, didn't it?"

"It did," he agreed gravely.

"Won't you tell me how it came into your possession?" she pleaded.

"I tell you I found it—that is true. I had no intention—" He stopped again. "It was—I picked it up in the road, in a country lane."

"But weren't you awfully surprised to find it, and didn't you tell the police?"

He shook his head.

"No," he said, "I was not surprised, and I did not tell the police, I intended restoring it; because, after all, jewels are of no value to me, are they?"

"I don't understand you, Gilbert."

She shook her head, a little bewildered. "Nothing is of any use except what belongs to you, is it?"

"That depends," he said, calmly. "But in this particular case I assure you that I brought this home tonight with the intention of putting it into a small box and addressing it to the Chief Commissioner of Police. You may believe that or not. That is why I thought it so extraordinary, when you were talking at dinner, that your mother should have lost a necklace, and that I should have found one."

They stood looking at one another, he weighing the necklace on the palm of his hand, tossing it up and down mechanically.

"What are we going to do with it now?" she asked. She was in a quandary. "I hardly know how to advise." She hesitated. "Suppose you carry out your present intention and send it to the police."

"Oh!" she remembered, with a little *moue* of dismay. "I have practically stolen three hundred pounds."

"Three hundred pounds!"

He looked at the jewel.

"It's worth more than three hundred pounds."

In a few words she explained how the jewel came to be lost, and how it came to be deposited in the hands of Warrell's.

"I'm glad to hear that your mother is the culprit. I was afraid you'd been gambling."

"Would that worry you?" she asked quickly.

"A little," he said; "it's enough for one member of a family to gamble."

"Do you gamble very much, Gilbert?" she asked seriously.

"A little," he said.

"Not a little," she corrected. "Stock Exchange business is gambling."

"I am trying to make money for you," he said brusquely. It was the most brutal thing he had said to her in her short period of married life, and he saw he had hurt her.

"I am sorry," he said gently. "I know I am a brute, but I did not mean to hurt you. I was just protesting in my heart against the unfairness of things. Will you take this, or shall I?"

"I will take it," she said, "But won't you tell the police where you found it? Possibly they might find the proceeds of other robberies near by."

"I think not," he replied with a little smile. "I have no desire to incur the anger of this particular gang. I am satisfied in my mind that it is one of the most powerful and one of the most unscrupulous in existence. It is nearly half-past ten," he said; "I must fly."

He held out his hand, and she took it. She held it for a moment longer than was her wont.

"Good-bye," she said. "Good luck, whatever your business may be."

"Thank you," he said.

She went slowly back to her guests. It did not make the position any easier to understand. She believed her husband, and yet there was a certain reservation in what he had told her, a reservation, which said as plainly as his guarded words could tell that there was much more he could have said had he been inclined.

She did not doubt his word when he told her that he had never stolen from—from whom was he going to say? She was more determined than ever to solve this mystery, and after her guests had gone she was busily engaged in writing letters. She was hardly in bed that night before she heard his foot on the stairs and listened. He knocked at her door as he passed.

"Good night," he said.

"Good night," she replied.

She heard his door close gently, and she waited for half an hour until she heard the click of his electric switch which told her that he was in bed, and that his light was extinguished.

Then she stole softly out of bed, wrapped her dressing-gown round her, and went softly down the stairs. Perhaps his coat was hanging in the hall. It was a wild, fantastic idea of hers that he might possibly have brought some further evidence that would help her in her search for the truth, but the pockets were empty.

She felt something wet upon the sleeve, and gathered that it was raining. She went back to her room, closed the door noiselessly, and went to the window to look out into the street. It was a fine morning, and the streets were dry. She saw her hands. They were smeared with blood!

She ran down the stairs again and turned on the light in the hall. Yes, there it was on his sleeve. There were little drops of blood on the stair carpet. She could trace him all the way up the stairs by this. She went straight to his room and knocked.

He answered instantly.

"Who is that?"

"It is I. I want to see you."

"I am rather tired," he said.

"Please let me in. I want to see you."

She tried the door, but it was locked. Then she heard the bed creak as he moved. An instant later the bolt was slipped, and the light shone through the fanlight over the door.

He was almost fully dressed, she observed.

"What is the matter with your arm?" she asked.

It was carefully bandaged.

"I hurt it. It is nothing very much."

"How did you hurt it?" she asked impatiently,

She was nearing the end of her resources. She wanted him to say that it had happened in a taxi-cab smash or one of the street accidents to which city dwellers are liable, but he did not explain.

She asked to see the wound. He was unwilling, but she insisted. At last he unwrapped the bandage, and showed an ugly little gash on the forearm. It was too rough to be the clean-cut wound of a knife or of broken glass.

There was a second wound about the size of a sixpence near the elbow.

"That looks like a bullet wound," she said, and pointed. "It has glanced along your arm, and has caught you again near the elbow."

He did not speak. She procured warm water from the bathroom and bathed it, found a cool emollent in her room, and dressed it as well as she could.

She did not again refer to the circumstances under which the injury had been sustained. This was not the time nor the place to discuss that.

"There is an excellent nurse spoilt in you," he said when she had finished.

"I am afraid there is an excellent man spoilt in you," she answered in a low voice; "and I am rather inclined to think that I have done the spoiling."

"Please get that out of your head altogether," he said almost roughly. "A man is what he makes himself: you know the tag—the evil you do by two and two you answer for one by one; and even if you had any part in the influencing of my life for evil, I am firstly and lastly responsible."

"I am not so sure of that," said she.

She had made him a little sling in which to rest his arm.

"You married me because you loved me, because you gave to me all that a right-thinking woman would hold precious and sacred, and because you expected me to give you something in return. I have given you nothing. I humiliated you at the outset by telling you why I had married you. You have the dubious satisfaction of knowing that I bear your name. You have, perhaps, half a suspicion that you live with one who is everlastingly critical of your actions and your intentions. Have I no responsibilities?"

There was a long silence, then she said:

"Whatever you wish me to do I will always do."

"I wish you to be happy, that is all," he replied. His voice was of the same hard, metallic tone which she had noted before.

She flushed a little. It had been an effort for her to say what she had, and he had rebuked her. He was within his rights, she thought.

She left him, and did not see him till the morning, when they met at breakfast. They exchanged a few words of greeting, and both turned their attention to their newspapers. Edith read hers in silence, read the one column which meant so much to her from end to end twice, then she laid the paper down.

"I see," she said, "that our burglars rifled the Bank of the Northern Provinces last night."

"So I read," he said, without raising his eyes from his paper.

"And that one of them was shot by the armed guard of the bank."

"I've also seen that," said her husband.

"Shot," she repeated, and looked at his bandaged arm.

He nodded.

"I think my paper is a later edition than yours," he said gently. "The man that was shot was killed. They found his body in a taxi-cab. His name is not given, but I happen to know that it was a very pleasant florid gentleman named Persh. Poor fellow," he mused, "it was poetic justice."

"Why?" she asked.

"He did this," said Gilbert Standerton, and pointed to his arm with a grim smile.

XI

The Fourth Man

On the night of Gilbert Standerton's little dinner party the black-bearded taxi-driver, who had called at the house off Charing Cross Road for instructions, came to the door of No. 43, and was duly observed by the detective on duty. He went into the house, was absent five minutes, and came out again, driving off without a fare.

Ten minutes later, at a signal from the detective, the house was visited by three C.I.D. men from Scotland Yard, and the mystery of the taxi-cab driver was cleared up forever.

For, instead of George Wallis, they discovered sitting at his ease in the drawing-room upstairs, and reading a novel with evident relish, that same black-bearded chauffer.

"It is very simple," said Inspector Goldberg, "the driver comes up and George Wallis is waiting inside, made up exactly like him. The moment he enters the door and closes it Wallis opens it, and steps out on to the car and drives off. You people watching thought it was the same driver returned."

He looked at his prisoner.

"Well, what are you going to do?" asked the bearded man.

"I am afraid there is nothing we can do with you," said Goldberg regretfully. "Have you got a licence?"

"You bet your life I have," said the driver cheerfully, and produced it.

"I can take you for consorting with criminals."

"A dfficult charge to prove," said the bearded one, "more difficult to get a conviction on, and possibly it would absolutely spoil your chance of bagging George in the end."

"That is true," said Goldberg; "anyway, I'm going to look for your taxi-cab. I can at least pull George in for driving without a licence."

The man shook his head.

"I am sorry to disappoint you," he said with mock regret, "but George has a licence too."

"The devil he has," said the baffled inspector.

"Funny, isn't it," said the bearded man. "George is awfully thorough."

"Come now, Smith," said the detective genially, "what is the game? How deep in this are you?"

"In what?" asked the puzzled man.

Goldberg gave him up for a bad job. He knew that Wallis had chosen his associates with considerable care.

"Anyway, I will go after George," he said. "You are probably putting up a little bluff on me about the licence. Once I get him inside the jug there are lots of little things I might be able to discover."

"Do," said the driver earnestly. "You will find him standing on the Haymarket rank at about half-past ten to-night."

"Yes, I know," said the detective sardonically.

He had no charge and no warrant, save the search warrant which gave him the right of entry.

Smith, the driver, was sent about his business, and a detective put on to shadow him.

With what success this shadowing was done may be gathered from the fact that, at half-past ten that night, Inspector Goldberg discovered the cab he was seeking, and to his amazement found it in the very place where Smith had told him to expect it. And there the bearded driver was sitting with all the aplomb of one who was nearing the end of a virtuous and well-rewarded day.

"Now, George," said the inspector jocularly, "come down off that perch and let me have a look at your licence; if it is not made out in your name I am going to pull you."

The man did not descend, but he put his hand in his pocket and produced a little leather wallet. The inspector opened it and read.

"Ah!" he said exultantly, "as I thought, this is made out in the name of Smith."

"I am Smith," said the driver calmly.

"Get down," said the inspector.

The man obeyed. There was no question as to his identity.

"You see," he explained, "when you put your flat-footed splits on to follow me I had no intention of bothering George. He is big enough to look after himself, and, by the way, his licence is made out in his own name, so you need not trouble about that.

"But as soon as I saw you did not trust me," he said reproachfully, "why, I sort of got on my mettle. I slipped your busy fellow in Oxford Street, and came on and took my cab from the desperate criminal you are chasing."

"Where is he now?" asked Goldberg.

"In his flat, and in bed I trust at this hour," said the bearded man virtuously. With this the inspector had to be content.

To make absolutely sure, he went back to the house off Charing Cross Road, and found, as he feared, Mr. George Wallis, if not in bed, at least in his dressing-gown, and the end of his silk pyjamas lapped over his great woollen slippers.

"My dear good chap," he expostulated wearily, "am I never to be left in quiet? Must the unfortunate record which I bear still pursue me, penitent as I am, and striving, as I may be, to lead that unoffending life which the State demands of its citizens?"

"Do not make a song about it, George," grumbled Goldberg. "You have kept me busy all the night looking after you. Where have you been?"

"I have been to a picture palace," said the calm man, "observing with sympathetic interest the struggles of a poor but honest bank clerk to secure the daughter of his rich and evil boss. I have been watching cowboys shooting off their revolvers and sheriffs galloping madly across plains. I have, in fact, run through the whole gamut of emotions which the healthy picture palace excites."

"You talk too much," said the inspector.

He did not waste any further time, and left Mr. Wallis stifling a sleepy yawn; but the door had hardly closed behind the detective when Wallis's dressing-gown was thrown aside, his pyjamas and woollen slippers discarded, and in a few seconds the man was full dressed. From the front window he saw the little knot of detectives discussing the matter, and watched them as they moved slowly to the end of the street. There would be a further discussion there, and then one of them would come back to his vigil; but before they had reached the end of the street he was out of the house and walking rapidly in the opposite direction to that which they had taken.

He had left a light burning to encourage the watcher. He must take his chance about getting back again without being observed. He made his way quickly in the direction of the tube station, and a quarter of an hour later, by judicious transfers, he was in the vicinity of Hampstead. He walked down the hill towards Belsize Park and picked up a taxi-cab. He had stopped at the station to telephone, and had made three distinct calls.

Soon after eleven he was met at Chalk Farm Station by his two confederates. Thereafter all trace was lost of them. So far, in a vague and unsatisfactory way, Inspector Goldberg had kept a record of Wallis's movements that night. He had to guess much, and to take something on trust, for the quarry had very cleverly covered his tracks.

At midnight the guard in the Bank of the Northern Provinces was making his round, and was ascending the stone steps which led from the vault below, when three men sprang at him, gagged him and bound him with incredible swiftness. They did not make any attempt to injure him, but with scientific thoroughness they placed him in such a position that he was quite incapable of offering resistance or of summoning assistance to his aid. They locked him in a small room usually occupied by the assistant bank manager, and proceeded to their work downstairs.

"This is going to be a stiff job," said Wallis, and he put his electric lamp over the steel grating which led to the entrance to the strong room.

Persh, the stout man who was with him, nodded.

"The grating is nothing," he said; "I can get this open."

"Look for the bells, Callidino," said Wallis.

The little Italian was an expert in the matter of alarms, and he examined the door scientifically.

"There is nothing here," he said definitely.

Persh, who was the best lock man in the world, set to work, and in a quarter of an hour the gate swung open. Beyond this, at the end of the passage, was a plain green door, offering no purchase whatever to any of the instruments they had brought. Moreover, the lock was a remarkable one, since it was not in the surface of the door itself, but in a small steel cabinet in the room overhead. But the blow-pipe was got to work expeditiously. Wallis had the plan of the door carefully drawn to scale, and he knew exactly where the vital spot in the massive steel covering was to be found. For an hour and a half they worked, then Persh stopped suddenly.

"What was that?" he said. Without another word the three men raced back along the passage, up the stairs to the big office on the ground floor, Persh leading.

As he made his appearance from the stairway a shot rang out, and he staggered. He thought he saw a figure moving in the shadow of the wall, and fired at it.

"You fool!" said Wallis, "you will have the whole place surrounded."

Again a shot was fired, and this time there was no doubt as to who was the assailant. Wallis threw the powerful gleam of his lamp in the direction of the office. With one hand free and the other holding a revolver, there crouched near the door the guard they had left secure. Wallis doused his light as the man fired again.

"Out of this, quick!" he cried. Through the back way they sped, up the little ladder, then through the skylight where they had entered, across the narrow ledge, and through the hosier's establishment which had been the means of entrance. Persh was mortally wounded, though he made the supreme and final effort of his life. They saw people running in the direction of the Bank, and heard a police whistle blow; but they came out of the hosier's shop together, quietly and without fuss, three respectable gentlemen, one apparently a little the worse for drink.

Wallis hailed a taxi-cab, and gave elaborate directions. He made no attempt to hurry whilst Callidino assisted the big man into the vehicle, then they drove off leisurely. As the cab moved Persh collapsed into one corner.

"Were you hit?" asked Wallis anxiously.

"I am done for, George, I think," whispered the man.

George made a careful examination with his lamp and gasped. He was leaning his head out of the window.

"What are you doing?" asked Persh, weakly.

"I am going to take you to the hospital," said Wallis.

"You will do nothing of the kind," said the other hoarsely. "For God's sake do not jeopardize the whole crowd for me. I tell you I am finished. I can—"

He said no other word, every muscle in his frame seemed at that moment to relax, and he slid in a loose heap to the floor.

They lifted him up.

"My God!" said Wallis, "he is dead."

And dead, indeed, was Persh, that amiable and florid man.

"The Burglary at the Northern Provinces Bank continues to excite a great deal of comment in City circles," wrote the representative of the *Daily Monitor*.

"The police have made a number of interesting discoveries. There can be no doubt whatever that the miscreants escaped by way of" (here followed a fairly accurate description of the method of departure). "What interests the police, however, is the evidence they are able to secure as to the presence of another man in the bank who is as yet unaccounted for. The fourth man seems to have taken no part in the robbery, and to have been present without the knowledge or without the goodwill of the burglars. The bank guard who was interviewed this morning by our representative, was naturally reticent in the interest of his employers, but he confirmed the rumour that the fourth man, whoever he was, was not antagonistic so far as he (the guard) was concerned. It now transpires that the guard had been hastily bound and gagged by the burglars, who probably, without any intention, had left their victim in some serious danger, as the gag had been fixed in such a manner that the unfortunate man nearly died.

"Then when he was almost *in extremis* there had appeared on the scene the fourth individual, who had loosened the gag, and made him more comfortable. It was obvious that he was not a member of the original burglar gang.

"The theory is offered that on the night in question two separate and independent sets of burglars were operating against the bank. Whether that is so or not, a tribute must be paid to the humanity of number four."

"So that was it." Wallis read the account in his paper that morning without resentment. Though the evening had ended disastrously for him, he had cause for satisfaction. "I should never have forgiven myself if we had killed that guard," he said to his companion.

His eyes were tired, and his face was unusually pale. He had spent a strenuous evening. He sat now in his bucket-shop office, and his sole companion was Callidino.

"I suppose poor old Persh will catch us," he said.

"Why Persh?" asked the other.

"The taxi-driver will be able to identify us as having been his companions. I wonder they have not come before. There is no use in running away. Do you know," he asked suddenly, "that no man ever escapes the English police if he is known. It saves a lot of trouble to await developments."

"I thought you had been to the station," said Callidino in surprise.

"I have," said Wallis; "I went there the first thing—in fact, the moment I had an excuse—to identify Persh. There is no sense in pretending we did not know him. The only thing to do is to prove the necessary alibis. As for me, I was in bed and asleep."

"Did anybody see you get back?" asked Callidino.

Wallis shook his head.

"No," he said; "they left one man to look after me, and he did a very natural thing, he walked up and down the street. There was nothing easier than to walk the way he was going behind his back and slip in just when I wanted to."

Shadowing is a most tiring business, and what very few realize is the physical strain of remaining in one position, having one object in view. Even the trained police may be caught napping in the most simple manner, and as Wallis said, he had found no difficulty in making his way back to the house without observation. The only danger had been that during his absence somebody had called.

"What about you?"

Callidino smiled.

"My alibi is more complex," he said, "and yet more simple. My excellent compatriots will swear for me. They lie very readily, these Neapolitans."

"Aren't you a Neapolitan?"

"Sicilian," smiled the other. "Neapolitan!"

The contempt in his tone amused Wallis.

"Who is the fourth man?" Callidino asked suddenly.

"Our mysterious stranger, I am certain of that," said George Wallis moodily. "But who the devil is he? I have never killed a man in my life so far, but I shall have to take unusual measures to settle my curiosity in this respect."

"There will have to be a division of the loot," he said after a while, "I will go into it today. Persh has relations somewhere in the world, a daughter or a sister, she must have her share. There is a fake solicitor in Southwark who will do the work for us. We shall have to invent an uncle who died."

Callidino nodded.

"As for me," he said, rising and stretching himself, "already the vineyards of the South are appealing to me. I shall build me a villa in Montecatini and drink the wines, and another on Lake Maggiore and bathe in the waters. I shall do nothing for the rest of my life save eat and drink and bathe."

"A perfectly ghastly idea!" said Wallis. The question of the fourth man troubled him more than he confessed. It was shaking his nerves. The police he understood, and was prepared for, could even combat, *but* here was the fourth man as cunning as they, who knew their plans, who followed them, who kept them under observation. Why? What object had he? He did not doubt that the fourth man was he who had watched them in Hatton Garden.

If it was a hobby it was a most extraordinary hobby, and the man must be mad. If he had an object in view, why did he not come out into the daylight and admit it?

"I wonder how I can get hold of him?" he said half aloud.

"Advertise for him," said Callidino. A sharp retort rose to the other's lips, but he checked it. After all, there was something in that. One could do many things through the columns of the daily press.

XII

The Place Where the Loot Was Stored

"Will The Hatton Garden intruder communicate with the man who lay on the floor, and arrange a meeting. The man on the floor has a proposition to make, and promises no harm to intruder."

Gilbert Standerton read the advertisement when he was taking his breakfast, and a little smile gathered at the corners of his lips. Edith saw the smile.

"What is amusing you, Gilbert?" she asked.

"A thought," he said. "I think these advertisements are so funny."

She had seen the direction of his eyes, carefully noted the page of the paper, and waited for an opportunity to examine for herself the cause of his amusement.

"By the way," he said carelessly, "I am putting some money to your credit at the bank today."

"Mine?" she asked.

He nodded.

"Yes, I have been rather fortunate on the Stock Exchange lately—I made twelve thousand pounds out of American rails."

She looked at him steadily.

"Do you mean that?" she asked.

"What else could I mean?" he demanded. "You see, American rails have been rather jumpy of late, and so have I."

He smiled again.

"I jumped in when they were low and jumped out when they were high. Here is the broker's statement."

He drew it from his pocket and passed it across the table to her.

"I feel," he said, with a pretence of humour, "that you should know I do not secure my entire income from my nefarious profession."

She made no response to this. She knew who the fourth man had been. Why had he gone there? What had been his object? If he had been a detective, or if he had been in the employ of the Government, he would have confessed it.

Her heart had sunk when she had read the interesting theory which had been put forward by the journal. He was the second burglar. She thought all this, with the paper he had passed to her on the table before her. The broker's statement was clear enough. Here were the amounts, all columns ruled and carried forward.

"You will observe that I have not put it all to your credit," he bantered; "some of it has gone to mine."

"Gilbert," she asked, "why do you keep things from me?"

"What do I keep from you?" he asked.

"Why do you keep from me the fact that you were in the bank the night before last when this horrible tragedy occurred?"

He did not answer immediately.

"I have not kept it from you," he said. "I have practically admitted it—in an unguarded moment, I confess, but I did admit it."

"What were you doing there?" she demanded.

"Making my fortune," he said solemnly.

But she was not to be put off by his flippancy.

"What were you doing there?" she asked again.

"I was watching three interesting burglars at work," he said, "as I have watched them not once but many times. You see, I am specially gifted in one respect. Nature intended me to be a burglar, but education and breed and a certain lawfulness of character prohibited that course. I am a dilettante: I do not commit crime, but I am monstrously interested in it. I seek," he said slowly, "to discover what fascination crime has over the normal mind; also I have an especial reason for checking the amount these men collect."

Her puzzled frown hurt him; he did not want to bother her, but she knew so much now that he must tell her more. He had thought it would have been possible to have hidden everything from her, but people cannot live together in the same house, and be interested in one another's comings and goings, without some of their cherished secrets being revealed.

"What I cannot understand—" she said slowly, and was at a loss for an introduction to this delicate subject.

"What cannot you understand?" he asked.

"I cannot understand why you suddenly dropped all your normal pleasures, why you left the Foreign Office, why you gave up music, and why, above all things, that this change in your life should have come about immediately after the playing of the 'Melody in F.'"

He was silent for a moment, and when he spoke his voice was low and troubled.

"You are not exactly right," he said. "I had begun my observations into the ways of the criminal before that tune was played."

He paused.

"I admit that I had some fear in my mind that sooner or later the 'Melody in F' would be played under my window, and I was making a half-hearted preparaation against the evil day. That is all I can tell you," he said.

"Tell me this," she asked as he rose, "if I had loved you, and had been all that you desired, would you have adopted this course?" He thought awhile.

"I cannot tell you," he said at length, "possibly I should, perhaps I should not. Yes," he said, nodding his head, "I should have done what I am doing now, only it would have been harder to do if you had loved me. As it is—"

He shrugged his shoulders.

He went out soon after, and she found the paper he had been reading, and without dificulty discovered the advertisement. Then he was the Hatton Garden intruder, and what he had said was true. He had observed these people, and they had known they were being observed. With a whirling brain she sat down to piece together the threads of mystery. She was no nearer a solution when she had finished, from sheer exhaustion, than when she had begun.

Gilbert had not intended spending the night away from his house. He realized that his wife would worry, and that she would have a genuine grievance; apart from which he was, in a sense, domesticated, and if the life he was living was an unusual one, it had its charm and its attraction. The knowledge that he would meet her every morning, speak to her during the day, and that he had in her a growing friend was particularly pleasing to him. He had gone to a little office that he rented over a shop in Cheapside—an office which his work in the City had made necessary.

He unlocked the door of the tiny room, which was situated on the third floor, and entered, closing the door behind him. There were one or two letters which had come to him in the capacity in which he appeared as the tenant of the office. They were mainly business communications, and required little or no attention. He sat down at his desk to write a note; he thought he might be late that night, and wanted to explain his absence. His wife occupied a definite place in his life, and though she exercised no rights over his movements, yet could quite reasonably expect to be informed of his immediate plans.

He had scarcely put pen to paper when a knock came to the door.

"Come in," said Gilbert, in some surprise.

It was not customary for people to call upon him here. He expected to see a wandering canvasser in search of an order, but the man that came in was nothing so commonplace. Gilbert knew him as a Mr. Wallis, an affable and a pleasant man.

"Sit down, will you?" he said, without a muscle of his face wrong.

"I want to see you, Mr. Standerton," said Wallis, and made no attempt to seat himself. "Would you care to come to my office?"

"I can see you here, I think," said Gilbert, calmly.

"I prefer to see you in my office," said the man, "we are less liable to interruption. You are not afraid to come, I suppose?" he said, with a hint of a smile.

"I am not to be piqued into coming, at any rate," smiled Gilbert; "but since this is not a very expansive office, nor conducive to expansive thought, I will go with you. I presume you intend taking me into your confidence?"

He looked at the other man strangely and Wallis nodded.

The two men left the office together, and Gilbert wondered exactly what proposition the other would put to him.

Ten minutes later they were in the St. Brides Street store, that excellent Safe Agency whose business, apparently, was increasing by leaps and bounds. Gilbert Standerton looked round.

The manager was there, a model of respectability. He bowed politely to Wallis, and was somewhat surprised to see him, perhaps, for the proprietor of the St. Bride's Safe Agency was a rare visitor.

"My office, I think?" suggested Wallis. He closed the door behind them.

"Now exactly what do you want?" asked Gilbert.

"Will you have a cigar?" Mr. Wallis pushed the box towards him.

Gilbert smiled.

"You need not be scared of them," said Wallis, with a twinkle in his eye. "There is nothing dopey or wrong with these, they are my own special brand."

"I do not smoke cigars," said Gilbert.

"Lie number one," replied Wallis cheerfully. "This is a promising beginning to an exchange of confidences. Now, Mr. Standerton, we are going to be very frank with one another, at least I am going to be very frank with you. I hope you will reciprocate, because I think I deserve something. You know so much about me, and I know so little about you, that it would be fair if we evened matters up."

"I take you," said Gilbert, "and if I can see any advantage in doing so you may be sure I shall act on your suggestion."

"A few months ago," said Mr. Wallis, pulling slowly at his cigar, and regarding the ceiling with an attentive eye, "I and one of my friends were engaged in a scientific work."

Gilbert nodded.

"In the midst of that work we were interrupted by a gentleman, who for a reason best known to himself modestly hid his features behind a mask." He shrugged his shoulders. "I deplore the melodrama, but I applaud the discretion. Since then," he went on, "the efforts of my friends in their scientific pursuit of wealth have been hampered and hindered by that same gentleman. Sometimes we have seen him, and sometimes we have only discovered his presence after we have retired from the scene of our labour. Now, Mr. Standerton, this young man may have excellent reasons for all he is doing, but he is considerably jeopardizing our safety."

"Who is the young man?" asked Gilbert Standerton.

"The young man," said Mr. Wallis, without taking his eyes from the ceiling, "is yourself."

"How do you know?" asked Gilbert quietly.

"I know," said the other with a smile, "and there is an end to it. I can prove it, curiously enough, without having actually spotted your face." He pulled an inkpad from the end of the desk. "Will you make a little finger-mark upon that sheet of paper?" he asked, and offered a sheet of paper. Gilbert shook his head with a smile.

"I see no reason why I should," he said coolly.

"Exactly. If you did we should find a very interesting finger-mark to compare with it. In the office here," Mr. Wallis went on, "we have a large safe which has been on our hands for some months."

Gilbert nodded.

"Owned by a client who has the keys," he said.

"Exactly," said Wallis. "You remember my lie about it. There are three sets of keys to that safe and a combination word. I said three"—he corrected himself carefully—"there are really four. By an act of gross carelessness on my part, I left the keys of the safe in my pocket in this very office three weeks ago."

"I must confess," he said with a smile, "that I did not suspect you of having so complete a knowledge of my doings or of my many secrets. I remembered my folly at eleven o'clock that night, and came back for what I had left behind. I found them exactly where I had left them, but somebody else had found them, too, and that somebody else had taken a wax impression of them. Moreover," he leant forward towards Gilbert, lowering his voice, "that somebody else has since formed the habit of coming to this place nightly for reasons of his own. Do you know what those reasons are, Mr. Standerton?"

"To choose a safe?" suggested Gilbert, ironically.

"He comes to rob us of the fruits of our labour," said Wallis.

He smiled as he said the words because he had a sense of humour. "Some individual who has a conscience or a sense of rectitude which prevents him from becoming an official burglar is engaged in the fascinating pursuit of robbing the robber. In other words, some twenty thousand pounds in solid cash has been taken from my safe."

"Borrowed, I do not doubt," said Gilbert Standerton, and leant back in his chair, his hands stuffed into his pockets, and a hard look upon his face.

"What do you mean—borrowed?" asked Wallis in surprise.

"Borrowed by somebody who is desperately in need of money; somebody who understands the Stock Exchange much better than many of the men who make a special study of it; somebody with such knowledge as would enable him to gamble heavily with a minimum chance of loss, and yet, despite this, fearing to injure some unfortunate broker by the accident of failure."

He leant towards Wallis, his elbow upon the desk, his face half averted from the other. He had heard the outer door close with a bang, and knew they were alone now, and that Wallis had designed it so.

"I wanted money badly," he said. "I could have stolen it easily. I intended stealing it. I watched you for a month. I have watched criminals for years. I know as many tricks of the trade as you. Remember that I was in the Foreign Office, in that department which had to do mainly with foreign crooks, and that I was virtually a police officer, though I had none of the authority."

"I know all about that," said Wallis. He was curious, he desired information for his own immediate use, he desired it, too, that his sum of knowledge concerning humanity should be enlarged.

"I am a thief—in effect. The reason does not concern you."

"Had the *'Melody in F'* anything to do with it?" asked the other dryly.

Gilbert Standerton sprang to his feet.

"What do you mean?" he asked.

"Just what I say," said the other, watching him keenly. "I understand that you had an eccentric desire to hear that melody played. Why? I must confess I am curious."

"Reserve your curiosity for something which concerns you," said the other, roughly. "Where did you learn?" he added the question, and Wallis laughed.

"We have sources of information—" he began magniloquently.

"Oh, yes," Gilbert nodded; "of course, your friend Smith lodges with the Wings. I had forgotten that."

"My friend Smith—you refer to my chauffeur, I suppose?"

"I refer to your confederate, the fourth member of your gang, the man who never appears in any of your exploits, and who in various guises is laying down the foundation for robberies of the future, Oh, I know all about this place," he said. He waved his hand around the shop, "I know this scheme of a Safe Agency; it is ingenious, but it is not original. I think it was done some years ago in Italy; you tout safes round to country mansions, offer them at ridiculous prices, and the rest is simple. You have the keys, and at any moment you can go into a house into which such a safe has been sold with the certain knowledge that all the valuables and all the portable property will be assembled in the one spot and accessible to you."

Wallis nodded.

"Quite right, friend," he said. "I need no information concerning myself. Will you kindly explain exactly what part you are taking? Are you under the impression that you are numbered amongst the honest?"

"I do not," said the other shortly. "The morality of my actions has nothing whatever to do with the matter. I have no illusion."

"You are a fortunate man," said George Wallis, approvingly. "But will you please tell me what part you are playing, and how you justify your action in removing from time to time large sums of money from our possession to some secret depository of your own?"

"I do not justify it," said Gilbert.

He got up and paced the little office the other watching him narrowly. "I tell you that I know that I am in intent a thief, but I am working to a plan."

He turned to the other. "Do you know that there is not a robbery you have committed of which I do not know the absolute effect? There is not a piece of jewellery you have taken, of which I do not know the owner and the exact value? Yes," he nodded, "I am aware that you have not 'fenced'—that is the term, isn't it?—a single article, and that in your safe place you have them all stored. I hope by good fortune not only to compensate you for what I have taken from you, but to return every penny that you have stolen."

Wallis started.

"What do you mean?" he asked.

"To its rightful owner," continued Gilbert calmly. "I have striven to be in a position to say to you: 'Here is a necklace belonging to Lady Dynshird, it is worth four thousand pounds, I will give you a fair price for it, let us say a thousand—it is rather more than you could sell it for—and we will restore it to its owner.' I want to say to you: 'I have taken ten thousand sovereigns in bullion and in French banknotes from your store, here is that amount for yourself, here is a similar amount which is to be restored to the people from whom it was taken.' I have kept a careful count of every penny you have taken since I joined your gang as an unofficial member."

He smiled grimly.

"My dear Quixote," drawled George Wallis protestingly, "you are setting yourself an impossible task."

Gilbert Standerton shook his head.

"Indeed I am not," he said. "I have made much more money on the Stock Exchange than ever I thought I should possess in my life."

"Will you tell me this?" asked the other. "What is the explanation of this sudden desire of yours for wealth—for sudden desire I gather it was?"

"That I cannot explain," said Gilbert, and his tone was uncompromising. There was a little pause, then George Wallis rose.

"I think we had better understand one another now," he said. "You have taken from us nearly twenty thousand pounds—twenty thousand pounds of our money swept out of existence."

Gilbert shook his head. "No, there is not a penny of it gone. I tell you I used it as a reserve in case I should want it. As a matter of fact, I shall not want it now," he smiled, "I could restore it to you to-night."

"You will greatly oblige me if you do," said the other.

Gilbert looked at him.

"I rather like you, Wallis," he said; "there is something admirable about you, rascal that you are."

"Rascals as we are," corrected Wallis. "You, who have no illusions, do not create one now."

"I suppose that is so," said the other moodily.

"How is this going to end?" asked Wallis. "Where do we share out, and are you prepared to carry on this high-soul arrangement as long as my firm is in existence?"

Standerton shook his head.

"No," he said, "your business ends to-night."

"My business?" asked the startled Wallis.

"Your business," said the other. "You have made enough money to retire on. Get out. I have made sufficient money to take over all your stock at valuation"—he smiled again—"and to restore every penny that has been stolen by you. I was coming to you in a few days with that proposition."

"And so we end to-night, do we?" mused Wallis. "My dear good man," he said cheerfully, "to-night—why I am going out after the most wonderful coup of all! You would laugh if you knew who was my intended victim."

"I am not easily amused in these days," said Gilbert. "Who is it?"

"I will tell you another time," said Wallis. He walked to the office door, his hands in his pockets. He stood for a moment admiring a huge safe and whistling a little tune.

"Don't you think it an excellent idea of mine," he asked with the casual air of the suburban householder showing off a new cucumber frame, "this safe?"

"I think it most excellent."

"Business is good," said Wallis regretfully. "It is a pity to give it up after we have taken so much trouble. You see, we may not sell half a dozen safes a year to the right kind of people, but if we only sell one— why we pay expenses! It is so simple," he said.

"By the way, have you missed a necklace of sorts which has been restored to the police? Do not apologize!"

He raised his hand.

"I understand this is a family matter. I am sorry to have caused you any inconvenience." His ironical politeness amused the other.

"It was not a question of family," he said. "I had no idea as to its ownership, only some person had been very careless—I found the necklace outside the safe. Some property had evidently been hidden in a hurry, and had fallen down."

"I am greatly obliged to you," said Wallis. "You removed what might possibly have been a great temptation for the honest Mr. Timmings."

He took a key from his pocket, switched round the combination lock and opened the safe. There was nothing in the first view to suggest that it was the storehouse of the most notorious thief in London. Every article therein had been most carefully wrapped and packed. He closed the door again.

"That is only half the treasure," he said.

"Only half—what do you mean?"

Gilbert was genuinely surprised, and a little mocking smile played about the mouth of the other.

"I thought that would upset you," he said. "That is only half. I will show you something. Since you know so much, why shouldn't you know all?"

He walked back into the office. A door led into another room. He unlocked this, and opening it passed through, Gilbert following. Inside was a small room lit by a skylight. The centre of the room was occupied by what appeared to be a large cage. It was in reality a steel grill, which is sometimes sold by French firms to surround a safe.

"A pretty cage," said Mr. Wallis, admiringly. He unlocked the tiny steel gate and stepped through, and Gilbert stepped after him.

"How did you get it in?" asked Gilbert curiously.

"It was brought in in pieces, and has just been set up in order to show a customer. It is very easily taken apart, and two or three mechanics can clear it away in a day."

"Is this your other department?" asked Gilbert, dryly.

"In a sense it is," said Wallis, "and I will show you why. If you go to the corner and pull down the first bar you will see something which perhaps you have never seen before."

Gilbert was halfway to the corner, when the transparency of the trick struck him. He turned quickly, but a revolver was pointed straight at his heart.

"Put up your hands, Mr. Gilbert Standerton," said George. "You may be perfectly *bona fide* in your intentions to share out, but I was thinking that I would rather finish to-night's job before I relinquish business. You see it will be poetic justice. Your uncle—"

"My uncle!" said Gilbert.

"Your uncle," bowed the other, "an admirable but testy old gentleman, who in one of our best safes has deposited nearly a quarter of a million pounds' worth of jewellery—the famous Standerton diamonds, which I suppose you will one day inherit."

"Is it not poetic justice," he asked as he backed his way out, still covering his prisoner with his revolver, "to rob *you* just a little? Possibly," he went on, with grim humour, "I also may have a conscience, and may attempt to restore to you the property which tonight I shall steal."

He clanged the gate to, doubly locked it, and walked to the door which led to the office."

"You will stay here for forty-eight hours," he said, "at the end of which time you will be released—on my word. It may be inconvenient for you, but there are many inconvenient happenings in this life which we must endure. I commend you to Providence."

He went out, and was gone for a quarter of an hour. Gilbert thought he had left, but he returned carrying a large jug of coffee, two brand-new quart vacuum flasks, and two packages of what proved to be sandwiches.

"I cannot starve you," he said. "You had better keep your coffee hot. You will have a long wait, and as you may be cold I have brought this."

He went back to the office and carried out two heavy overcoats and, thrust them through the bars.

"That is very decent of you," said Gilbert.

"Not at all," said the polite Mr. Wallis.

Gilbert was unarmed, and had he possessed a weapon it would have been of no service to him. The pistol had not left Wallis's hand, and even as he handed the food through the grill the butt of the automatic Colt was still gripped in his palm.

"I wish you a very good evening. If you would like to send a perfectly non-committal note to your wife, saying that you were too busy to come back, I should be delighted to see it delivered."

He passed through the bars a sheet of paper and a stylograph pen. It was a thoughtful thing to do, and Gilbert appreciated it.

This man, scoundrel as he was, had nicer instincts than many who had never brought themselves within the pale of the law. He scribbled a note excusing himself, folded up the sheet and placed it in the envelope, sealing it down before he realized that his captor would want to read it.

"I am very sorry," he said, "but you can open it, the gum is still wet."

Wallis shook his head.

"If you will tell me that there is nothing more than I asked you to write, or that I expected you to write, that is sufficient," he said. So he left Gilbert alone and with much to think about.

XIII

THE MAKER OF WILLS

G eneral Sir John Standerton was a man of hateful and irascible temper. The excuse was urged for him that he had spent the greater portion of his life in India, a country calculated to undermine the sweetest disposition. He was a bachelor and lived alone, save for a small army of servants. He had renamed the country mansion he had purchased twenty years before: it was now known from one end of the country to the other as The Residency, and here he maintained an almost feudal state.

His enemies said that he kept his battalion of servants at full strength so that he might always have somebody handy to swear at, but that was obviously spite. It was said, too, that every year a fresh firm of solicitors acted for him, and it is certain that he changed his banks with extraordinary rapidity.

Leslie Frankfort was breakfasting with his brother one morning in his little Mayfair house. Jack Frankfort was a rising young solicitor, and a member of that firm which at the moment was acting for Sir John Standerton.

"By the way," said Jack Frankfort, "I am going to see an old friend of yours this afternoon."

"Who is my old friend?"

"Old Standerton."

"Gilbert?"

Jack Frankfort smiled.

"No, Gilbert's terrible uncle; we are acting for him just now."

"What is the object of the visit?"

"A will, my boy; we are going to make a will."

"I wonder how many wills the old man has made?" mused Leslie. "Poor Gilbert!"

"Why poor Gilbert?" asked the other, helping himself to the marmalade.

"Why, he was his uncle's heir for about ten minutes."

Jack grinned. "Everybody is old Standerton's heir for ten minutes," he said. "I verily believe he has endowed every hospital, every dog's home, every cat's home every freakish institution that the world has ever heard of, in the course of the last twenty years, and he is making another will to-day."

"Put in a good word for Gilbert," said Leslie with a smile. The other growled. "There is not a chance of putting in a good word for anybody. Old Tomlins, who acted for him last, said that the greater difficulty in making a will for the old beggar is to finish one before the old man has thought out another. Anyway, he is keen on a will just now, and I am going down to see him. Come along?"

"You know the old gentleman?"

"Not on your life," said the other hastily.

"I know him indeed, and he knows me! He knows I am a pal of Gilbert's. I stayed once with him for about two days. For the Lord's sake do not confess that you are my brother, or he will find another firm of solicitors."

"I do not usually boast of my relationship with you," said Jack.

"You are an offensive devil," said the other admiringly. "But I suppose you have to be, being a solicitor."

John Frankfort journeyed down to Huntingdon that afternoon in the company of a pleasant man, with whom he found himself in conversation without any of that awkwardness of introductions which makes the average English passenger so impossible. This gentleman had evidently been in all parts of the world, and knew a great many people whom Jack knew. He chatted interestingly for an hour on the strange places of the earth, and when the train drew up at the little station at which Mr. Frankfort was alighting, the other accompanied him.

"What an extraordinary coincidence," said the stranger heartily. "I am getting out here too. This is a rum little town, isn't it?"

It might be described as "rum," but it was very pleasant, and it contained one of the most comfortable hostelries in England. The fellow-passengers, found themselves placed in adjoining rooms. Jack Frankfort had hoped to conclude his business before the evening and return to London by a late train, but he knew that it would be unwise to depend upon the old man's expedition.

As a matter of fact, he had hardly been in the hotel a quarter of an hour before he received an intimation from The Residency that Sir John could not be seen until ten o'clock that evening.

"That settles all idea of going back to London," said Jack, despairingly.

He met his fellow-passenger at dinner. Though he was not particularly well acquainted with the habits of Sir John, he knew that one of his fads was to dine late, and since he had no desire to spend a hungry evening, he advanced the normal dinner-hour of the little hotel by thirty minutes. He explained this apologetically to the comfortable man who sat opposite him, as they discussed a perfectly roasted capon.

"It suits me very well," said the other, "I have a lot of work to do in the neighbourhood. You see," he explained, "I am the proprietor of the Safe Agency."

"Safe Agency," repeated the other, wonderingly.

The man nodded.

"It seems a queer business, but it is a fairly extensive one," he said. "We deal principally in safes and strong rooms, second-hand or new. We have a pretty large establishment in London; but I am not going to overstep the bounds of politeness"—he smiled—"and try to sell you some of my stock."

Frankfort was amused.

"Safe Agency," he said; "one never realizes that there can be money in that sort of thing."

"One cannot realize that there is money in any branch of commerce," said the other. "The money-making concerns which appeal are those where one sees brains being turned into actual cash."

"Such as—?"

"Such as a lawyer's business," smiled the other. "Oh, yes, I know you are a lawyer, you are the type, and I should have known your trade if I had not seen your dispatch case, and then your name."

Jack Frankfort laughed. "You are sharp enough to be a lawyer yourself," he suggested.

"You are paying yourself a compliment," said the other.

Later, in the High Street, when he was calling a fly to drive him to The Residency, Jack noticed a big covered motor lorry, bearing only the simple inscription on its side: "The St. Bride's Safe Company." He saw also his pleasant companion speaking earnestly with the black-bearded chauffeur. A little later the lorry moved on through the narrow streets of the town and took the London Road.

Jack Frankfort had no time to speculate upon the opportunities for safe-selling which the little town offered, for five minutes later he was in Sir John Standerton's study.

The old General was of the type which is frequently depicted in humorous papers. He was stout and red of face, and wore a close-cut strip of white whisker, which ended abruptly below his ear, and was continued in a wild streak of white moustache across his face. He was bald, save for a little fringe of white hair which ran from temple to temple via the occiput, and his conversation might be described as a succession of explosions.

He stared up from under his ferocious eyebrows, as the young man entered the study, and took stock of him. He was used to lawyers. He had had every variety, and had divided them into two distinct classes— they were either rogues or fools. There was no intermediate stage with this old man, and he had no doubt in his mind that Jack Frankfort, a shrewd-looking young man, was to be classed in the former category.

He bullied him into a seat.

"I want to see you about my will," he said. "I have been seriously thinking lately of rearranging the distribution of my property."

This was his invariable formula. It was intended to convey the impression that he had arrived at this present state of mind after very long and careful consideration, and that the making of wills was a serious and an important business to be undertaken, perhaps, once or twice in a man's lifetime.

Jack nodded.

"Very good, General," he said. "Have you a draft?"

"I have no draft," snapped the other. "I have a will which has already been prepared, and here is a copy." He threw it across to his solicitor.

"I do not know whether you have seen this?"

"I think I have one in my bag," said Jack.

"What the devil do you mean by carrying my will about in your bag?" snarled the other.

"That is the only place I could think of," said the young man, calmly. "You would not like me to carry it about in my trousers' pocket, would you?"

The General stared. "Do not be impertinent, young man," he said ominously.

It was not a good beginning, but Jack knew that every method had been tried, from the sycophantic to the pompous, hut none had succeeded, and the end of all endeavours, so far as the solicitors were concerned, had been the closing of their association with the General's estate. He was rather a valuable client if he could only be retained. No human solicitor had discovered a method of retaining him.

"Very well," said the general at last. "Now please jot down exactly what my wishes are, and have the will drafted accordingly. In the first place I revoke all former wills."

Jack, with a sheet of paper and a pencil, nodded and noted the fact. "In the second place I want you to make absolutely certain that not a penny of my money goes to Dr. Sundle's Dogs' Home. The man has been insolent to me, and I hate dogs, anyhow. Not a penny of my money is to go to any hospital or to any charitable institution whatever."

The old sinner declaimed this with relish.

"I had intended leaving a very large sum of money to a hospital fund," he explained, "but after the behaviour of this infernal Government—" Jack might have asked in what way the old man expected to get even with the offending Government by denying support to all institutions designed to help the poor, but wisely kept the question in the background.

"No charitable institution whatever." The old man spoke slowly, emphatically, thumping the table with every other word.

"A hundred pounds to the Army Temperance Association, though I think it is a jackass of an institution. A hundred pounds to the Soldiers' Home at Aldershot, and a thousand pounds if they make it non-sectarian."

He grinned and added: "It will be Church of England to everlasting doomsday, so that money's safe! And," he added, "no money to the Cottage Hospital here—do not let that bequest creep in. That stupid maniac of a doctor—I forget his beastly name—led the agitation for opening a right-o'-way across my estate. I will 'right-o'-way' him!" he said viciously.

He spent half an hour specifying the people who were not to benefit by his will, and the total amount of his reluctant bequests during that period did not exceed a thousand pounds. When he had finished he stared hopelessly at the young lawyer, and a momentary glint of humour came in the hard old blue eyes.

"I think we have disposed of everybody," he said, "without disposing of anything. Do you know my nephew?" he asked suddenly.

"I know a friend of your nephew."

"Are you related to that grinning idiot Leslie Frankfort?" roared the old man.

"He is my brother," said the other, calmly.

"Humph," said the General, "I thought I recognized the face. Have you met Gilbert Standerton?" he asked suddenly.

"I have met him once or twice," said Jack Frankfort carelessly, "as you may have met people, just to say 'how do you do?' and that sort of thing."

"I have never met people to say 'how do you do?' and that sort of thing," protested the old man with a snort. "What sort of fellow do you think he is?" he asked after a pause.

The injunction of Leslie to "say a good word for Gilbert" came to the young man's mind.

"I think he is a very decent sort of fellow," he said, "though somewhat reserved and a little stand-offish."

The old man glowered at him.

"My nephew stand-offish?" he snapped, "of course he is stand-offish. Do you think a Standerton is everybody's money? There is nothing Tommyish or Dickish or Harryish about our family, sir. We are all stand-offish, thank God! I am the most stand-offish man you ever met in your life."

"That I can well believe," thought Jack, but did not give utterance to his thought. Instead he pursued the subject in his own cunning way. "He is the sort of man," he said, innocently, "whom I should think money would be rather wasted on."

"Why?" asked the General with rising wrath.

Jack shrugged his shoulders. "Well, he makes no great show, does not attempt to keep any particular place in London Society. In fact, he treats Society as though he were superior to it."

"And so he is," growled the General, "we are all superior to Society. Do you think, sir, that I care a damn about any of the people in this country? Do you think I am impressed by my Lord of High Towers and my Lady of the Grange, and the various upstart parvenu aristocrats that swarm over this country like—like—field mice? No, sir! And I trust my nephew is in the same mind. Society, as it is at present constituted, is not worth that!"

He snapped his fingers in Jack's impassive face.

"That settles it," said the General with decision. He pointed his finger at the notes which the other was taking. "The residue of my property I leave to Gilbert Standerton. Make a note of that."

Twice had he uttered the same words in his lifetime, and twice had he changed his mind. It might well be that he would change his mind again. If the reputation he bore was justified, the morning would find him in another frame of mind.

"Stay over to-morrow," he said at parting. "Bring me the draft at breakfast time."

"At what hour?" asked Jack, politely.

"At breakfast time," roared the old man.

"What is your breakfast hour?"

"The same hour as every other civilized human being," snapped the General, "at twenty-five minutes to one. What time do you breakfast, for Heaven's sake?"

"At twenty to one," said Jack, sweetly, and was pleased with himself all the way back to the hotel.

He did not see his train companion that night, but met him at breakfast the next morning at the Christian hour of half-past eight. Something had happened in the meantime to change the equable and cheery character of the other. He was sombre and silent, and he looked worried, almost ill, Jack thought. Possibly there was a bad time for safe-selling, as there was a bad time for every other department of trade.

Thinking this, he kept off the subject of business, and scarcely half a dozen sentences were exchanged between the two during the meal. Returning to The Residency, Jack Frankfort found with surprise that the old man had not changed his mind overnight. He was still of the same opinion; seemed more emphatically so. Indeed, Jack had the greatest difficulty in preventing him from striking off a miserable hundred pounds bequest which he had made to a northern dispensary.

"The whole of the money should be kept in the family," said the General shortly; "it is absurd to fritter away little hundreds like this, it handicaps a man. I do not suppose he will have the handling of the money for many years yet, but 'forethought,' sir, is the motto of our family."

It was all to Gilbert's advantage that the lawyer persisted in demanding the restoration of the dispensary bequest. In the end the General cut out every bequest in the will, and in the shortest document which he had ever signed bequeathed the whole of his property, movable and immovable, to "my dear nephew" absolutely.

"He is married, isn't he?" he asked.

"I believe he is," said Jack Frankfort.

"You believe! Now what is the good of your believing?" protested the old man. "You are my lawyer, and your business is to know everything. Find out if he is married, who his wife is, where she came from, and ask them up to dinner."

"When?" demanded the startled lawyer.

"To-night," said the old man. "There is a man coming down from Yorkshire to see me, my doctor, we will make a jolly party. Is she pretty?"

"I believe she is." Jack hesitated, for he was honestly in doubt. He knew very little about Gilbert Standerton or his affairs.

"If she is pretty and she is a lady," said the old General slowly, "I will also make provision for her, separately."

Jack's heart sank. Would this mean another will?

For good or ill, the wires were dispatched. Edith received hers and read it in wonder. Gilbert's remained on the hall table, for he had not been home the previous night nor during that day. The tear-reddened eyes of the girl offered eloquent testimony to the interest she displayed in his movements.

XIV

THE STANDERTON DIAMONDS

E dith Standerton made a quick preparation for her journey. She would take her maid into Huntingdon, and go without Gilbert. It was embarrassing that she must go alone, but she had set herself a task, and if she could help her husband by appearing at the dinner of his irritable relative she would do so.

She had her evening things packed, and caught the four o'clock train for the town of Tinley.

The old man did her the exceptional honour of meeting her at the station.

"Where is Gilbert?" he asked, when they had mutually introduced themselves.

"He has been called out of town unexpectedly," she said. "He will be awfully upset when he knows."

"I think not," said the old General grimly. "It takes a great deal to upset Gilbert—certainly more than an opportunity of being reconciled to a grouchy old man. As a matter of fact," he went on, "there is no reconciliation necessary; but I always look upon anybody whom I have to cut out of my will as one who regards me as a mortal enemy."

"Please never put me in your will." She smiled.

"I'm not so sure about that," said he, and added gallantly, "though I think Nature has sufficiently endowed you to enable you to dispense with such mundane gifts as money!"

She made a little face at that.

He was delighted with her, and found her a charming companion. Edith Standerton exerted herself to please him. She had a style of treating people older than herself in such a way as to suggest that she was as young as they. I do not know any other phrase which would more exactly convey my meaning than that. She had a charm which appealed to this wayward old man.

Edith did not know the cause of the change in her husband's fortunes. She knew very little, indeed, of his affairs; enough she knew that for some reason or other he had been disinherited through no fault of his own. She did not even know that it was the result of a caprice of this old man.

"You must come again and bring Gilbert," said the General, before they dispersed to dress for dinner. "I shall be delighted to put you both up."

Fortunately, she was saved the embarrassment of an answer, for the General jumped up suddenly.

"I know what you'd like to see," he said, "you'd like to see the Standerton diamonds, and so you shall!"

She had no desire to see the Standerton diamonds, had, indeed, no knowledge that such an heirloom existed; but he was delighted at the prospect of showing her; and she, being a woman, was not averse to a view of these precious jewels, even though she were not destined to wear them.

He led the way up to the library, and Jack Frankfort followed.

"There they are," said the old man proudly, and pointed to a big safe in the corner—a large and ornate safe.

"That is something new," he said proudly. "I bought it from a man who wanted sixty guineas for it—an infernal, swindling, travelling rascal! I got it for thirty. What do you think of that for a safe?"

"I think it's very pretty," said Jack. He could think of nothing more fitting.

The old man glared at him. "Pretty!" he growled. "What do you think I want with 'pretty' things in my library?"

He took a bunch of keys from his pocket and opened the door of the safe; pulled open a drawer, and took out a large morocco case.

"There they are!" he said with pride, and indeed he might well be proud of such a beautiful collection. With all a girl's love for pretty things Edith handled the gorgeous jewels eagerly. The setting was old-fashioned, but it was the old fashion which was at that moment being copied. The stones sparkled and glittered as though every facet carried a tiny electric lamp to send forth the green, blue and roseate gleam of its fire. Even Jack Frankfort, no great lover of jewellery, was fascinated by the sight.

"Why, sir," he said, "there are nearly a hundred thousand pounds' worth of gems there."

"More," said the old man. "I've a pearl necklace here," and he pulled out another drawer, "look at it. There is nearly two hundred thousand pounds' worth of jewellery in that safe."

"In a thirty-guinea safe," said Jack unwisely.

The old man turned on him. "In a sixty-guinea safe," he corrected violently "Didn't I tell you I beat the devil down? I beg your pardon, my dear."

He chuckled at the thought, replaced the jewels, and locked the safe again. "Sixty guineas he wanted. Came here with all his fine City of London manner, frock-coat, top-hat, and patent boots, my dear. The way these people get up is scandalous. He might have been a gentleman by the airs he gave himself."

Jack looked at the safe. He had some ideas of commercial values.

"I can't understand how he sold it," he said. "This safe is worth two hundred pounds."

"What?" The old General turned on his lawyer in astonishment.

Jack nodded.

"I have one at my office, now that I come to think of it," he said. "It cost two hundred and twenty pounds, and it is the same make."

"He only asked me sixty guineas."

"That's strange. Do you mind opening it again? I'd like to see the bolts."

The General, nothing loath, turned the key and pulled open the huge door. Jack looked at the square, steel bolts—they were absolutely new.

"I can't understand how he offered it for sixty. You certainly had a bargain for thirty, sir," he said.

"I think I have," said the General, complacently. "By the way, I am expecting a man to dinner to-night," he went on, as he led the way back to the drawing-room, "a doctor man from Yorkshire—Barclay-Seymour. Do you know him?"

Jack did not know him, but the girl broke in: "Oh, yes, he is quite an old friend of mine."

"He's rather a fool," said the General, adopting his simple method of classification.

Edith smiled. "You told me yesterday that there were only two classes of people, General—rogues and fools I am wondering," she said demurely, "in which class you place me."

The old man wrinkled his brows. He looked at the beautiful young face in his high good humour.

"I must make a new class for you," he said. "No, you shall be in a class by yourself. But since most women are fools—"

"Oh, come!" she protested, laughingly.

"They are," he averred. "Look at me. If women weren't fools shouldn't I have had a wife? If any brilliant, ingenious lady, possessed of the necessary determination had pursued me and had cultivated me, I should not be a bachelor, leaving my money to people who don't care two—pins," he hastily substituted a milder phrase for the one he had intended, "whether I'm alive or dead. Does your husband know the Doctor, by the way?"

The girl shook her head.

"I don't think so," she said. "They nearly met one night at dinner, but Gilbert had an engagement."

"But Gilbert knows him," insisted the old man. "I've often talked to him about Barclay-Seymour, who, by the way, is perhaps not such a fool as most doctors. I used to be rather more enthusiastic about him than I have been lately," he admitted, "and I'm afraid I used to ram old Barclay-Seymour down poor Gilbert's throat, more than his ability or genius justified me doing. Has he never spoken about him?"

The girl shook her head.

"Ungrateful devil!" growled the old General, inconsequently.

One of his many footmen came into the drawing-room at that moment with a telegram on a salver.

"Hey, hey?" demanded Sir John, fixing his glasses on the tip of his nose and scowling up at his servant. "What's this?"

"A telegram, Sir John," replied the footman.

"I can see it's a telegram, you ass! When did it come?"

"A few minutes ago, sir."

"Who brought it?"

"A telegraph boy, Sir John," said the imperturbable servitor.

"Why didn't you say so at first?" snapped Sir John Standerton in a tone of relief. And Edith had all she could do to prevent herself from bursting into a fit of laughter at the little scene.

The old man opened the telegram, spread it out, read it slowly and frowned. He read it again. "Now, what on earth does that mean?" he asked, and handed the telegram to the girl. She read:

"Take the Standerton jewels out of your safe and deposit them without fail in your bank to-night. If it is too late to send them to your bank place them under an armed guard."

It was signed "Gilbert Standerton."

XV

The Tale the Doctor Told

The General read the telegram again. He was, despite his erratic temperament, a shrewd and intelligent man.

"What does that mean?" he asked, quietly for him. "Where is Gilbert? And where does he wire from?"

He picked up the telegram and inspected it. It was handed in at the General Post Office at London at 6.35 P.M.

The General's hour for dining was consonant with his breakfast hour, and it was a quarter after nine when the dinner gong brought Edith Standerton down from her room. She was worried; she could not understand the reference to the jewels. What had made Gilbert send this message? Had she known more of the circumstances of what had happened on the previous afternoon, she would have wondered rather how he was able to send the message.

The General took the warning seriously, but not so seriously that he was prepared to remove his jewellery to any other receptacle. Indeed, the purchase of the safe had been made necessary by the fact that, beyond the butler's strong room, which was strong only in an etymological sense, there was no security for property of any value.

He had made an inspection of the jewels in the safe and had relocked the door, leaving a servant in the library, with strict instructions not to come out until he was instructed to leave by his master.

Edith came down to find that another guest had arrived, a guest who greeted her with a cheery and familiar smile.

"How do you do, Doctor?" she said.

"It is not so long since I met you at mother's. You remember me?"

"I remember you perfectly," said Dr. Barclay-Seymour. He was a tall, thin man with a straggling iron-grey beard and a high forehead. A little absent in his manner, he conveyed the impression, never a very flattering one, that he had matters more weighty to think about than the conversation which was being addressed to him. He was, perhaps, the most noteworthy of the provincial doctors.

He came out of his shell sufficiently to recognize her and to remember her mother. Mrs. Cathcart had been a great friend of Barclay's. They had grown up together.

"Your mother is a very wonderful woman," said Dr. Barclay-Seymour as he took the girl in to dinner, "a remarkable woman."

Edith was seized with an almost overwhelming temptation to ask why. It would have been unpardonable of her had she done so, but never did a word so tremble upon a human being's lips as that upon hers.

They ate through dinner, which was made a little uncomfortable by the fact that General Sir John Standerton was unquestionably nervous. Twice during the course of the meal he sent out one of the three footmen who waited at table to visit what he termed the outpost. Nothing untoward had happened on either occasion.

"I do not know what to do about this jewellery. I hope that Gilbert is not playing the fool," he said.

He turned to Edith with a genial scowl.

"Has he developed any kittenish ways of late?"

She smiled.

"There is no word which less describes Gilbert than kittenish," she said.

"Is it not remarkable that he sent that message?" the General went on testily. "I hardly know what to do. I could get a constable up, but the police here are the most awful and appalling idiots. I have a great mind to have my bed put in the library and sleep there myself."

He brightened up at the thought. He had reached the stage in life when sleeping in any other room than that to which he was accustomed represented a form of heroism.

After the dinner was through, they made their way to the drawing-room. The General was fidgety, and though Edith played and sang a little French love-song with no evidence of agitation, she was as nervous as the General.

"I will tell you what we will do," said Sir John suddenly, "we will all adjourn to the library. It is a jolly nice room if you do not mind our smoking."

It was an excellent suggestion, and one that she accepted with pleasure. She was the only lady of the party, and remarked on the fact as she went upstairs with Sir John. He glanced hurriedly round.

"I always regard a doctor as a fit chaperone for any lady," he said with a chuckle—it amused him. Later he found the complement of the joke, and discoursed loudly upon old women of all professions, a discourse which was arrested by the arrival of the Doctor and Jack Frankfort.

The library was a big room, and it was chiefly remarkable for the fact that it contained no more evidence of Sir John's literary taste than a number of volumes of the *Encyclopedia Britannica* and a shelf full of *Ruff's Guide to the Turf.* It was, however, a delightful room, panelled in old oak with mullioned windows standing in deep recesses. These, explained Sir John, opened out on to a terrace—an excellent reason for his apprehension.

"Pull the curtain, William," said Sir John to the waiting footman, "and then you can clear out. Have the coffee brought in here." The man pulled the heavy velvet curtains across the big recesses, placed a chair for the girl, and retired.

"Excuse me," said Sir John. He went across to the safe and opened it again. He inspected the case. Nothing had been disturbed.

"Ah," he breathed—It was a sigh of infinite relief. "This wire of Gilbert's is getting on my nerves," he excused himself, irritably. "What the devil did he wire for? Is he the sort of man that sends telegrams to save himself the bother of licking down an envelope?"

Edith shook her head.

"I am as much in the dark as you," she said, "but I assure you that Gilbert is not an alarmist."

"How do you get on with him?" he asked her.

The girl flushed a little.

"I get on very well," she said, and strove to turn the conversation. But it was a known fact that no human soul had ever turned Sir John from his set inquisitional course.

"Happy, and that sort of thing?" he asked. Edith nodded, keeping her eyes on the wall behind the General's head.

"I suppose you love him—hey?"

Edith was embarrassed, and no less so were the two men; but Sir John was not alone in imagining that doctors have little sense of decency, and lawyers no idea of propriety. They were saved further discussion by the arrival of coffee, and the girl was thankful.

"I am going to keep you here until Gilbert comes up for you," said the old man suddenly. "I suppose you know, but probably you do not, that you are the first of your sex that I have ever tolerated in my house."

She laughed.

"It is a fact," he said seriously. "You know I do not get on with women. They do not realize that, though I am an irritable old chap, there is really no harm in me, and I *am* an irritable old chap," he confessed. "It is not that they are impertinent or rude, but it is their long-suffering meekness that I cannot stand. If a lady tells me to go to the devil I know where I am. I want the plain, blunt truth without gaff. I prefer my medicine without sugar."

The Doctor laughed.

"You are different from most people, Sir John. I know men who are rather sensitive about the brutal truth."

"More fools they," said Sir John.

"I do not know," said the Doctor, reflectively. "I sympathize with a man who does not want the whole bitterness of fact hurled at his head in the shape of an honest half a brick, although there is an advantage in knowing the truth; sometimes, it saves a lot of needless unhappiness," he added, a little sadly. He seemed to have aroused some unpleasant train of thought.

"I will give you an extraordinary instance," he went on, in his usual deliberate manner. "What's that?" asked the General suddenly.

"I think it was a noise in the hall," said Edith.

"I thought it was a window," growled the General, rather ashamed that he should have been detected in his jump. "Go on with your story, Doctor."

"A few months ago," Dr. Seymour recalled, "a young man came to me. He was a gentleman, and evidently not a townsman of Leeds, at any rate I did not know him. I found afterwards that he had come from London to consult me. He had some little tooth trouble a jagged molar, a very commonplace thing, and he had made a slight incision in the inside of his mouth. Apparently it worried him, the more so when he discovered that the tiny scratch would not heal. Like most of us, he had a terrible dread of cancer."

He lowered his voice as a doctor often will when he speaks of this most dreadful malady.

"He did not want to go to his own doctor; as a matter of fact, I do not think he had one. He came to me, and I examined him. I had my doubts as to there being anything wrong with him, but I cut a minute section of the membrane for microscopic examination."

The girl shivered. "I am sorry," said the Doctor hastily, "that is all there is in the story which is gruesome, unless you think—However," he went on, "I promised to send him the result of my examination, and I wanted his address to send it. This, however, he refused. He was very, very nervous. 'I Know I am a moral coward,' he said, 'but somehow I do not want to know just the bare truth in bald language; but if it is as I fear, I would like the news broken to me in the manner which is the least jarring to me.'"

"And what was that?" asked Sir John, interested in spite of himself. The Doctor drew a long breath.

"It seems," he said, "that he was something of a musician"—Edith sat upright, clasping her hands, her face set, her eyes fixed upon the Doctor—"he was something of a musician, that is to say, he was very keen on music, and the method he had of breaking the news to himself was unique, I have never heard anything quite like it before in my life. He gave me two cards and an addressed envelope, addressed to an old musician in London whom he patronized."

Edith saw the room go swaying round and round, but held herself in with an effort. Her face was white, her hands that held the chair were clenched so tightly that the bones shone white through them.

"They were addressed to an old friend of his, as I say, and they were identically worded with this exception. One of them, said in effect, you will go to such and such a place and you will play the '*Melody in F*,' and the other gave the same instructions but varied to this extent, that he was to play the '*Spring Song.*' Now here comes the tragedy."

He raised his finger. "He gave me the '*Melody in F*' to signal to him the fact that he had cancer."

There was a long silence which only the quick breathing of the girl broke.

"And, and—?" whispered Edith.

"And"—the Doctor looked at her with his faraway eyes—"I sent the wrong card," he said. "I sent it and destroyed the other before I remembered my error."

"Then he has not cancer?" whispered the girl.

"No, and I do not know his address, and I cannot get at him," said Barclay-Seymour.

"It was tragic in many ways. I think he was just going to marry, for he said this much to me: 'If this is true, and I am married, I will leave my wife a pauper,' and he asked me a curious question," added the Doctor.

"He said, 'Don't you think that a man condemned to die is justified in taking any action, committing any crime, for the protection of the loved ones he leaves behind?'"

"I see," said Edith. Her voice was hollow, and sounded remote to her.

"What is that?" said the General, and jumped up.

This time there was no doubt. Jack Frankfort sprang to the curtain that covered the recess and pulled it aside.

There stood Gilbert Standerton, white as a ghost, his eyes staring into vacancy, the hand at his mouth shaking.

"The wrong card!" he said. "My God!"

XVI

BRADSHAW

A month later, Gilbert Standerton came back from the Foreign Office to his little house in St. John's Wood.

"There is a man to see you, Gilbert," said his wife.

"I think I know, it is my bank manager," he said. He greeted the tall man who rose to meet him with a cheery smile.

"Now, Mr. Brown," he said, "I have to explain to you exactly what I want done. There is a man in America, he has been there some week or two, to whom I owe a large sum of money—eighty thousand pounds, to be exact—and I want you to see that I have sufficient fluid capital to pay it."

"You have quite sufficient, Mr. Standerton," said the manager, "even now, without selling any of your securities."

"That is good. You will have all the particulars here," said Gilbert, and took a folded sheet of paper from his pocket. "It is really a trust, in the sense that it is to be transferred to two men, Thomas Black and George Smith. They may sub-divide it again, because I believe," he smiled, "they have other business associates who happen to be entitled to share."

"I did not congratulate you, Mr. Standerton," said the bank manager, "upon the marvellous service you rendered the City. They say that, through you, every penny which was stolen by the famous Wallis gang has been recovered."

"I think that pretty well described the position," said Gilbert, quietly.

"I was reading an account of it in a paper the other day," the bank manager went on. "It was very providential that there was an alarm of fire next door to their headquarters."

"It was providential that it was found before the fire reached the Safe Company's premises," said Gilbert. "Fortunately the firemen saw me through the skylight. That made things rather easy, but it was some time before they got me out, as you probably know."

"Did you ever see this man Wallis?" asked the hank manager, curiously.

"Didn't the papers tell you that?" bantered Gilbert with a dry smile.

"They say you learnt in some way that there was to be a burglary at your uncle's, and that you went up to his place, and there you saw Mr. Wallis under the very window of the library, on the parapet or something."

"On the terrace it was," said Gilbert, quietly.

"And that he flew at sight of you?"

"That is hardly true," said Gilbert, "rather put it that I persuaded him to go. I was not sure that he had not already secured the necklace, and I went through the window into the room without realizing there was anybody there. You see, there were heavy curtains which hid the light. Whilst I was there he escaped, that is all."

He made one or two suggestions regarding the transfer of the money and showed the bank manager out, then he joined Edith in the drawing-room. She came to him with a little smile.

"Does the Foreign Office seem very strange to you?" she asked.

"It did seem rather strange after my other exploits."

He laughed.

"I never thought Sir John had sufficient influence to get you back."

"I think he has greater influence than you imagine," he said; "but then there were other considerations. You see, I was able to render the Foreign Office one or two little acts of service in the course of my nefarious career, and they have been very good."

She looked at him, wistfully.

"And do we go back now to where we started?" she asked.

"Where did we start?" he countered.

"I do not know that we started anywhere," she said, thoughtfully.

She had been looking at a time-table when he came into the room, and now she picked it up and turned the pages idly.

"Are you interested in that Bradshaw?"

"Very," she said. "I am just deciding."

"Deciding what?" he asked.

"Where—where we shall spend our honeymoon," she faltered.

A Note About the Author

Edgar Wallace (1875–1932) was an English novelist, journalist, and short story writer. Born in London, Wallace—then named Richard Horatio Edgar Freeman—was raised by George and Clara Freeman, a fishmonger and his wife who adopted the boy from his mother Polly Richards, an actress. The Freeman family, despite being semi-literate, endeavored to provide Wallace with a good education, allowing him to rise above a youth mired in poverty. Wallace left school at the age of twelve to enter the workforce, finding employment as a newspaper-seller, factory worker, and milkman. At twenty-one, he joined the British Army under the name "Edgar Wallace" and was sent to South Africa that same year. After meeting Rudyard Kipling in Cape Town in 1898, Wallace embarked on a career as a writer, first with a book of ballads and then as a war correspondent covering the Boer War for Reuters and the *Daily Mail*. He returned to London in 1903, impoverished and in dire need of providing for his young family. Over the next several years, he earned money with detective stories before establishing his own press to publish his books, starting with *The Four Just Men* (1905). Between 1908 and 1932, Wallace became a popular and prolific novelist and story writer, eventually moving to Hollywood to work as a script doctor, an industry term used for writers hired to polish or even rewrite an existing script. In 1931, Wallace began developing the script for the classic 1933 film *King Kong*, released the year after his death.

A Note from the Publisher

Spanning many genres, from non-fiction essays to literature classics to children's books and lyric poetry, Mint Edition books showcase the master works of our time in a modern new package. The text is freshly typeset, is clean and easy to read, and features a new note about the author in each volume. Many books also include exclusive new introductory material. Every book boasts a striking new cover, which makes it as appropriate for collecting as it is for gift giving. Mint Edition books are only printed when a reader orders them, so natural resources are not wasted. We're proud that our books are never manufactured in excess and exist only in the exact quantity they need to be read and enjoyed.

Discover more of your favorite classics with Bookfinity™.

- Track your reading with custom book lists.
- Get great book recommendations for your personalized Reader Type.
- Add reviews for your favorite books.
- AND MUCH MORE!

Visit **bookfinity.com** and take the fun Reader Type quiz to get started.

Enjoy our classic and modern companion pairings!

Printed in the USA
CPSIA information can be obtained
at www.ICGtesting.com
JSHW082357140824
68134JS00020B/2132